Love Unveiled...

Julia's body was aflame as Brad's taut form touched her. Once again his tongue sought hers. Her lips were still warm and moist. His hands began to trace the outline of her soft tender curves. They moved languidly from her throat to her breast, brushing her taut nipple, then gliding down to her smooth thighs. Her flesh tingled at his touch. She twisted her body to feel more of him, wrapping her arms tightly around his neck. Julia thought, at last. The picture had come to life. He is real and more than I imagined. She felt as though she were drowning, then again, flying, high into the sky. Her emotions soared at these new and delightful sensations. Soared as high as the birds that suddenly began calling to one another. The high pitched sound invaded Julia's senses. Pushing her hands against Brad's chest, she sat up. "Brad. What are we doing? I'm sorry . . . Samantha . . . I–I– I don't know . . ."

The following titles in the Indigo Series are available through Genesis Press:

Entwined Destinies by Rosalind Welles

Everlastin' Love by Gay G. Gunn

Here and Now by Francine Clark-Garcia

Dark Storm Rising by Chinelu Moore

Shades of Desire by Monica White

Reckless Surrender by Susan James

Careless Whispers by Rochelle Alers

Breeze by Robin Lynette Hampton

Whispers in the Sand by LaFlorya Gaunthier

Love Unveiled by Gloria Greene

Love's Deceptions by Charlene Berry

See our World Wide Web page for our newest releases and other infomation.

Genesis OnLine: http://www.colom.com/genesis

Acknowledgements

For my husband . . .

whose love and support is priceless . . .

and fo r all my family and friends who cheered me on.

Tear off the veil — you will find my heart exposed.

—*Rutheda Feusner*

INDIGO STORIES are published by
The Genesis Press, Inc.
406A Third Avenue North
Columbus, MS 39703-0101

LOVE UNVEILED

Published in the United States of America by The Genesis Press, Inc. For information Address: The Genesis Press, Inc., 406A 3rd Ave N., Columbus, MS 39703-0101.

ISBN: 1-885478-08-9

Manufactured in the United States of America

First Edition

Love Unveiled

Gloria Greene

The Genesis Press, Inc.
406A Third Avenue N
Columbus, MS 39703-0101

Chapter I

The Virginia air at high noon was hot, humid and muggy. Julia Hart had removed the lightweight cotton jacket she'd worn on the plane as covering in the air-conditioned cabin. Now, standing in line at the notions counter in the lobby of Norfolk International Airport waiting for her rental car, she pulled at the clammy cotton V-neck T-shirt. As the line inched up, she thumbed lazily through the fashion magazine she was waiting to purchase.

"She's an American, you know. She was interviewed on 'Oprah' with some other models a few months ago."

"Yeah, I'd heard she was from the States. Which one? Do you know?"

The two young women ahead of Julia in the line were enviously staring at the beautiful model on the cover of *Sans*–the same magazine Julia was waiting to purchase.

"I don't know," the first girl said, her eyes searching the cover, studying every detail of the pretty face. "I missed the first part of the show." She sighed. "I wonder how she got her break? And in France." She heaved another long sigh. "I wish it was me."

Her friend, devouring her own copy, said dreamily, "And that name–Sammí–that's *workin'*." She looked yearningly at the picture. "I think I'll use one name too when I'm discovered.

It's so. . . so mysterious."

Julia smiled to herself as she eavesdropped on the conversation of the two teens. They left the counter, still chattering about their own dream careers. When she reached the counter, the young man raised a brow as he looked at the magazine. "Umm. Three in a row. She's really selling that mag this month, isn't she?" he said to Julia, his face splitting into a friendly grin. "Who is she?" he added curiously. "She's a beauty."

As Julia pocketed her change, taking her purchase and refusing a bag, she answered, "Her name is Sammí," putting the accent on the 'i'. "She's been the hottest model in Paris for the past few years. Apparently the States have just discovered her," Julia said dryly. The young man grinned again as Julia began to walk away.

"Figures," he said, shaking his head, turning his attention to the next customer.

Tucking the magazine under her arm, she walked the few steps to the car rental booth. As she approached, the agent held out the keys. "Your car is ready, Ms. Hart. Enjoy your stay in Norfolk," she said.

Easily handling her nylon overnight bag, following the agent's directions, Julia headed out into the heavy, moist heat. She found the shiny, red Shadow with no problem. Tossing her bag on the passenger seat, she climbed in and started the engine. Liking the sound and feel of it, she nodded in satisfaction as she tooled her way out of the airport.

Once out of the complex and on Military Highway, she relaxed and began to enjoy the drive to her parents' home in Hampton Roads. She had worked feverishly the past few weeks in order to make this year's family reunion, a tradition in the Hart family since Julia was a child growing up in Norfolk. She had missed last year's and heard her mother reminding her for weeks afterward about the importance of family and staying in touch. She had managed to tie up loose ends at *Rags*, a fashion magazine in New York City. As associate art director, she had to review all selections being considered for the fall issue and make her recommendations to the senior associate art director. Fashions, models and sitting dates were all in place, awaiting final approval. She had left the office late last night exhausted, but satisfied.

Earlier she had told her boss she'd see him in a month and not to expect her back before August. The next morning she caught the early morning flight out of La Guardia Airport.

She smiled as she thought about the two envious teenagers at the airport a few minutes ago fantasizing about becoming like the beautiful model, Sammí, who was Julia's younger sister, Samantha Hart. For the last five years she was the top runway and fashion model in Paris. The past two years she had been appearing more frequently in American magazines, making the cover of three of them in one month. The reunion this July would be Samantha's first in three years. She'd spoken excitedly to Julia by phone a week ago: "I can finally make it this year, Ju— it'll be great seeing you and Mom and Dad—and guess what. Brad is coming. You can finally meet my Brad!"

Julia absently ran long slender fingers through her jet black cap of twisted and crinkled ringlets. She frowned, thinking of the man, Brad, who was accompanying Sam home. Sam never mentioned that this was a serious relationship—but does one bring a man from France, just to attend a big backyard party? Julia's frown deepened, causing her brilliant, black, doe-shaped eyes to glint contemplatively. "Brad is so moody," Julia could hear Sam's breathless voice. "He is like a chameleon. But we get along just fine. We're good together." Good together? What did she mean by that? This Brad, Julia thought, he sounds so strange–not at all the man she would pick for Samantha. Uh, oh, Julia, be careful, she told herself. She smiled. Once a big sister. . . She had to remind herself that little Samantha, Sammí, France's darling, was all grown up at twenty-four. Julia knew she was acting over-protective, but she felt responsible. After all, there would be no Sammí if Julia hadn't coaxed Sam into posing for a class assignment. With her professor's help she had submitted the photo to an international competition. A star was born.

As she drove, the excitement of seeing Sam again after so long was building. She told herself that her feelings about the reunion were genuine, not that she was simply interested in meeting Samantha's mystery man, the man her letters always mentioned. Last year, Sam had sent a picture of happy, laughing people crowded around a swimming pool. "Brad's in this one, Ju," she'd written. Julia had looked at the picture and instantly knew Brad. His eyes were magnetic. She had caught her breath as she stared.

Although he was in the group, he was not a part of it. Her eyes roamed over the tall, masculine form. Her pulse quickened as her eyes traveled from his bare feet, taking in the muscled legs—another breath—her eyes hurriedly moved to the lean stomach, broad chest, and that enigmatic face. His wide mouth was spread generously in a grin that showed even, white teeth. His eyes seemed to hold Julia's. The smile was a lie, for it never reached those unfathomable ebony eyes above high cheekbones. They stared back at Julia, dark and cold. "I know you, Brad." A tiny smile played at the corners of Julia's mouth as she recalled that moment. She had startled herself when she had heard the sound of her voice. Going crazy girl—watch it—talking to the picture of a man you've never met . . . and such a haughty one at that, she thought.

Now, as Julia neared the home of her childhood, she thought that finally she would meet Mr. Brad whatever his name was and see what he has in mind for our Sam. She nodded her head firmly. "You'd better be all that she thinks you are, Mister. That's all I've got to say," she said aloud. A sudden surge of warmth coursed through her body at the thought of coming face-to-face with her sister's friend. She shook her head in annoyance at the now-familiar sensation she felt whenever his image danced before her. "What's wrong with me? I've never met the man."

She pulled the car into the crowded driveway of her parents' home. The D.C. crowd had arrived, she observed, looking at the various license plates, South Carolina, North Carolina, New York—New York? Who's here from New York besides me? she wondered.

"Julia, Julia. Julia's here. Julia, take my picture?"

"No, take my picture, Julia."

Julia grinned, her dark eyes twinkling as she braced herself for the onslaught of hugging and kissing from two roly-poly nine-year-old cousins, Jamal and Austin. They were identical twins and she could never tell them apart.

"Now you know, you guys are my favorite subjects and you're both going to get so tired of posing that you're going to run when you see me coming at you," she teased. It was a family bet on who was going to be the next member to be made famous by one of her photographs.

"No, we won't, Cousin Julia. You'll see." Laughing, they all stumbled up the front door steps where Julia was hugged by her mother and greeted by numerous cousins and other relatives who were already engaged in various activities. Some were in the kitchen fussing with dishes of food, some were quieting crying children and Julia could see from the kitchen window that some of the men were fumbling with the tangles of the volleyball net.

"Oh M'Dear," Julia said, using the childhood name for her mother, "it's just like it was when I was growing up, only there's more of everybody. Is Sam here yet? Where's Dad?"

Frieda Hart laughed as she looked at her beautiful daughter. Shaking her head, she wondered where all the years had gone. Her eyes misted as she remembered Julia and Samantha when they were young and underfoot at family gatherings. Now, standing before her was this vibrant young woman, so unaware of her good looks, chattering away like the twins.

Julia's soft black cap of curls shone with the moisture of the July heat, causing little ringlets to stray. Her dark eyes danced with excitement. How nice to see her this happy, thought Frieda, knowing that Julia presented a reserved exterior to some people, as if the facade were used as protection against some sort of invasion. Frieda had observed this change in her daughter's personality while Julia was still attending college. After Julia had assured her that everything was fine—health, grades—Frieda never spoke about the quiet moods again, attributing them to the maturing process of a young college woman.

"Ju—Ju," squealed Samantha.

Julia turned in time to be pounced upon by a tall, leggy, giggling bronze creature.

"Is this the sophisticated model, France's darling?" laughed Julia, squeezing her younger sister in a bear hug. As they spun one another around, Julia's eyes locked with those of the bemused stranger leaning casually against the kitchen door, filling the entrance with his huge frame.

Brad, thought Julia, and that same warm sensation sped through her body as it had when she'd gazed at his picture. She pulled her eyes away, as Sam's voice penetrated her thoughts.

"Shoot, Julia! You're beautiful! From the way you wrote about how tired you looked, I was prepared for the worse. . . and ready to use my magic creams to pretty you up. M'Dear, you think she might be trying to give me some competition?" Releasing Julia, Samantha turned to her mother with her dazzling smile.

"Well, Mademoiselle Sammí," said a smiling Frieda in her very best French accent, "I would certainly be the proudest mother in all of Hampton Roads with two famous models as my daughters, if Mademoiselle Julia chose to work in front of the cameras instead of behind them," joked Frieda. She ended with a burst of laughter and Julia and Samantha joined her.

In the midst of the merriment, a deep voice said, "I'll drink to that, Frieda."

"Oh," Samantha said. "Brad, come meet my sister Julia. Julia, this is Brad Coleman. You know this is only a formality because you both know all about one another. I swear Brad, Julia gets bent out of shape with me mentioning you all the time. I don't know why." She looked at Julia, saying, "Poor Brad. He listened to my chatter about my big sister so patiently." Tucking her arm in Brad's while looking up at him adoringly, she said, "But he didn't mind. He's my special person."

Julia, hearing those words, suddenly felt strangely lonely. So he is special to her, she thought. But why do I feel so down about it? she asked herself. I should be happy that Sam has fallen in love. She seems so happy, Julia observed. Snapping out of her sudden somber mood, remembering her manners, Julia extended her hand and in her best company voice and smile said, "Hello, Mr. Coleman. Nice to meet you."

"Julia," squeaked Samantha in a burst of laughter that doubled her over, "This is Brad, my Brad, remember? Mr. Coleman, indeed. He's going to be family."

"Now, Sam, your sister is only minding her manners as you should be, young lady," admonished Frieda in a mock-stern voice.

"Well, well," George Hart said as he entered the kitchen. "Here are all my ladies." A stocky, balding man with a booming voice, he turned to Brad. "You've gotten their attention I see," he remarked, grinning as he walked towards Julia with outstretched arms. "Hi, babykins. How's my favorite daughter?"

Everyone laughed. Frieda, noting the quizzical look on Brad's face said, "Family joke, Brad. George always called them both his 'favorite girl' but they each became jealous every time. To stop the bickering he got a brainstorm. He greets each one as his oldest and youngest "favorite" daughter. Since that's exactly what they are, there's no argument." Frieda smiled at her husband, placing an arm around his ample middle.

"Daddy never answers when I ask him what if two more daughters came along," quipped Samantha.

With an embarrassed grunt at the attention he was receiving, George said, "Food, ladies, food. People are banging on the tables now. Everything ready?"

"Almost, almost," Frieda said, pushing a bowl of green salad into his hands. "Here, take this. More's coming. Here, Sam," she said, pushing a basket full of fresh baked rolls to her. "Brad, you can handle these." She gave him a stack of gaily-colored plastic plates and cups. Taking a tray of fried chicken, Frieda started out the door, calling over her shoulder, "Julia, honey, would you finish up that sinkful of salad greens? I'll be back for the ham—" her voice trailed away with the slam of the screen door.

"I'm fine, Ms. Hart, and how are you?"

Julia jumped at the sound of his voice. He spoke to her as if nothing had occurred since her first stilted greeting to him and now he was waiting for her response.

Brad stood gazing at Julia, his dark eyes full of naked admiration as they boldly traveled from her tawny shoulders down her slender body to her slim, sandled feet and upward again to blazing dark eyes. She's more lovely than I'd imagined, he thought.

He is so close, Julia thought, becoming acutely conscious of his maleness. She took a quick step backward as if in flight—from what she did not know. She was annoyed at the confusion she felt. She stared at Brad, saying pointedly, "I'm Julia, you're Brad—for Sam's sake," she added, turning to the sink and attacking a head of lettuce.

"For Sam's sake," she heard Brad echo softly, as he left to deliver the plates.

Why, he was actually kissing me with his eyes, she thought in astonishment. But the man in the picture—his eyes were so cold. And now, here in the flesh, those eyes were making love to me. She flushed at the thought because she was not too annoyed at the idea. Does he turn hot and cold at will? she wondered. Is that what Sam had meant about her "moody" friend? At the thought of Samantha, Julia frowned, feeling guilty about her feelings toward Brad, feelings that long ago she'd buried deep inside, allowing no man to bring them to the surface. Now, she shook her head with impatience. Stop it, she told herself, you're just curious about this stranger who means so much to your little sister. She tried not to think about the many times during the past year she'd gazed at Brad's picture, experiencing strange and delightful sensations. Feelings long buried had come alive—over a photograph. Frightened at the thoughts that danced in her head, she would hide the picture, only to ferret it out from its secret place in her lingerie drawer. Only weeks before her planned trip home and the eventual meeting of Brad, Julia had suddenly realized that she was falling in love with a man she'd never met.

Lost in these disturbing thoughts, Julia felt a soft breeze on the nape of her neck that sent shivers down to her toes. Turning, she saw Brad, who had softly blown a wayward ringlet of her hair.

"You're beautiful," Brad whispered. "I couldn't resist that." Julia, black eyes flashing, drew herself up to her full height of five-feet-seven, which was not nearly enough to look Brad in the eye without tilting her head back.

"Mr. Coleman," she bristled, "I'm not in the habit of letting men caress my neck, guest in my mother's house or not," she finished emphatically.

"Is that what you felt?" Brad drawled.

"What?"

"Did you really feel a caress?" The smile that split his face reached his eyes.

Staring into those jet-black twinkling pools, she felt as though she were being drawn into their depths. With great difficulty she struggled to regain her composure.

"If—if—I—oh, you're exasperating," she blurted, confused by the delicious quiver rippling down her spine. She was flabbergasted at her inability to speak sensibly in this man's presence, she who managed and controlled a staff of twenty professionals with deft precision.

Breaking from the hypnotic gaze, swinging back to the sink, she picked up the bowl of lettuce and pushed it into his hands. "Here. Make yourself useful. Take this to my mother, please. You can do that, can't you?" she asked in a steadier voice.

Moving dangerously close to her, he breathed into her ear, "Yes, pretty lady, for you, I can do that." He smiled wickedly, turned, and smoothly eased his firmly-muscled body from the room.

Reaching for the carving knife, she pulled the plate of ham toward her and winced as the blade nicked the tip of her thumb. Who is he? She marvelled at the sureness of his matter, the devil-may-care look in his eyes, the tingling of her flesh when she felt his soft breath. Her mind raced, not believing her feelings.

"Why, I actually *wanted* him to touch me," she exclaimed to the empty room.

Chapter II

The house had long since settled. Brad lay on the bed in the darkened room listening to the night sounds. The cacophony of the crickets piercing the warm air had awakened him. He opened his eyes slowly, quickly focusing on his surroundings, a polished practice, honed from years of travel. Still dressed, he lay on his back, stockinged feet crossed at the ankles, head resting on clasped hands. He realized his intended five-minute rest had stretched into hours, for the luminous dial of his watch showed it was well past two in the morning. After the guests had gone, final family chatter shared, rooms assigned and goodnights said, he'd lain down, waiting his turn to use the hall bathroom. Amidst the sounds of running water and the whispers and giggles made by Julia and Samantha who were sharing the next bedroom, he'd dozed off, succumbing to jet lag. He had flown from Paris to New York and a day later had driven to Virginia.

With the thought of Julia sleeping so near, Brad frowned at the slight quiver that started in his stomach and quickly descended to his loins. Moving his head as if to shake away unwanted memories, he closed his eyes. "No," he muttered, "it will not happen again. I will not allow it to happen again."

The short frilly white curtains danced playfully as warm breezes drifted through the screened windows. Rising silently,

Brad walked to the window, sat on the cushioned seat in the alcove and gazed into the dark. Absently, as he watched passing fireflies light patches of darkness, his thoughts drifted to the events of the day. They were thoughts of Julia. Julia, Julia, they hummed.

When he first saw her in the kitchen, laughing and hugging Samantha, aware of her beautiful smile and musical laugh, his breath got tangled up in his throat. Though he appeared to be a nonchalant onlooker, his insides were churning like a ship's rudder. Unnoticed, he watched as the playful exchange with her parents and sister unabashedly revealed her natural warmth and humor.

Her vibrant dark eyes held a constant smile. Until she saw him. When her eyes locked with his, the smile was replaced with a puzzled stare. When Samantha formally introduced them, Julia's demeanor changed drastically. Instead of warmth radiating from her handshake, he felt as if a cloud had descended over them both and shed droplets of cold rain. The moment was brief and unnoticed by the others, yet when they were left alone in the kitchen he noticed not coldness but confusion and, strangely, something he thought to be dismay. From gay to somber in a flash. But through it, he detected her attraction to him. Yet she tried to hide it under a veil of dislike. He wondered if this was not yet another ploy by a beautiful woman applying Rule No. 6 of a "How to Get your Man" article.

Through Samantha, he had learned Julia was single and lived alone. Romantic involvements he didn't know of, but he had observed the opal and gold ring she wore on her third finger, left hand. A lover's gift? The thought caused his brow to furrow because, according to Sam, although it was her favorite gemstone, Julia believed purchasing opals for oneself brought bad luck. Brad had spent many hours in Paris listening to the lonely model, Sammí, as Parisians called her, talk about her family in far away America. Now, watching the silent darkness, he remembered the effect Julia had on him. The sweet muskiness of her flushed skin had sent his pulse spinning, and he could not deny that the feelings of desire welling up in his body were beginning to stir his soul, feelings he'd not allowed himself to have for a woman in six years, feelings left untouched by his female companions over the years though a few tried in earnest to reach his core. But for Julia—in the space of a day, his heart had begun to ache. Brad left the window embrasure, took off his pants and shirt and, lying naked on the bed except for his briefs, stared into the dark. He turned his head to look at the wall separating the two bedrooms. His hoarse whisper invaded the silence. "Julia, are you only another Laura?"

"Good morning, Brad." said Frieda. "Come in and have a cup of coffee with me before you leave for the breakfast party. I'm afraid our girl Sam's left you. She said Julia would show you the way to Cousin Caroline's."

"Oh, she did, did she?" fumed Julia, who had overheard her mother's words. She had showered and dressed and was approving her appearance in the upstairs foyer cheval mirror, glad she had chosen the white shorts and V-neck violet halter with matching sandals, because already she could feel the early morning heat that promised to turn the day into a scorcher. She patted her curls and was walking down the stairs when she heard her mother's voice.

Entering the kitchen, she greeted her mother, planting a kiss on Frieda's cheek. "Good morning, Brad," she said, as he stood to help her onto her chair at the table. At his touch, Julia inwardly winced, trying to ignore the quiver in her stomach.

Feeling Brad's eyes on her, Julia forced herself to look at the magnetic man seated across from her. He was staring at her in open admiration, allowing his eyes to travel to the deep V of her halter and slide slowly to her neck, her mouth, her eyes. His whole face smiled at her, from the cool black eyes to the moustached mouth where Julia allowed her eyes to rest lingeringly. To her embarrassment, Brad caught her stare. She wondered if he could read her thoughts at the moment—that she longed to feel his lips caress her neck.

Almost in answer to her silent question, Brad gazed intensely at Julia's neck, his black eyes dancing. Frieda, noticing this byplay, tactfully rose and left the kitchen to "wake up the sleepy household."

"And why didn't you leave with Sam?" Julia said, in a tone she hoped conveyed her annoyance at having to accompany Brad to the brunch. Brad lifted his gaze to Julia's eyes as he said, "Oh, you know our Samantha. She's tireless. She's so happy to be home that she wants to see everybody, make all the parties, do it all, so she can take the memories back to Paris. I warned her beforehand when she invited me that I was not *about* to try to keep up."

"Then we'd better get started," Julia said. "We don't want to keep missing her, do we?" she smiled sweetly.

As they left the house, Julia started toward her rented car while Brad headed for the bright red Cougar with the New York plates.

"Oh," exclaimed Julia, "but I thought—oh, never mind. You can drive, I know the way."

Brad eased the sleek car down the driveway and onto the quiet Sunday street following Julia's travel directions. After a few moments of silence, Brad spoke softly. "What did you think, Julia?" he said.

"About what?"

"My New York plates. You were startled."

"But don't you live in Paris with my, uh, mmm . . . don't you live in Paris?" Julia finished.

"I travel a lot, Julia. My business takes me to many cities, Paris is one of them, but my home is in New York City."

"But, Sam, how. . . " Julia's voice trailed away.

"I met Samantha on one of my trips. We've been friends ever since," Brad said firmly.

"We intended to leave Paris together," Brad continued, "but a business emergency forced me to leave two days earlier than I had planned. I promised Samantha that I'd be with her this weekend, so I decided to drive. I needed the hours to think," he ended, his expression becoming grim, his hands tightening on the steering wheel.

Julia, noting the set line of his mouth, did not speak, but turned to watch the road. She was silent, reflecting on her unusual behavior. In the space of twenty-four hours her usual take-charge manner and calm reserve had evaporated in the presence of this intriguing stranger who so boldly displayed his desire for her. Even more unsettling, this stranger was her sister's lover, an invited guest in her parents' home and Frieda Hart appeared not to mind Brad's attention to her oldest daughter!

Feeling more flustered than ever, Julia gave her attention to the passing scenery. They had turned off the main highway at Julia's direction and were driving on a quiet road along the Hampton River. Julia always loved this drive because commercialism had not yet snapped up this five-mile stretch of grass, trees and woodland that was still only sparsely populated with private residences and businesses.

Occasionally, a whiff of freshly-cut grass and the faint sounds of a mower reached Julia. She loved the sounds and smells of summer, especially summer in New York. She had given up long ago trying to explain this phenomenon to her friends. But the bustle and sounds of New York never failed to either excite, amuse, anger, stimulate, gladden or bewilder her. As a "people" person, summer enabled her to see, hear and observe more of them, her camera at the ready. In keeping with her habit as a college student, she rarely left her apartment without one of her many cameras.

In New York, life and death dramas played all around her on any given day. A screaming siren could mean a rush to save a life or the same sound could herald the arrival of a newborn. On one block, a whiff of barbecue watered the mouth, while around the corner the smell of burning cinders assailed the nostrils. For the past several months Julia's interest in trees and flowers, the clouds in the sky, rock formations and anything and everything natural had consumed her recreational picture-taking. After long and exhaustive photo sessions with beautiful models, Julia found nature shooting relaxing. She often joked that a tree didn't talk back, fidget or require touch-ups.

"Stop the car, please," Julia said. Without hesitation, Brad pulled the car over, smoothly bringing it to a halt along a deserted grassy knoll. Clutching the camera she had picked up before leaving the house, Julia slid from the car and quickly ran up the gently-sloped hill. Focusing her camera, she began capturing the panoramic view before her; the rolling hills; the still river reflecting the clear blue sky and sparkling sun; the purple milkweed wildflowers called pokeweed with their vain display of pink and white crowns blowing softly to and fro as if dancing to unheard music.

"Beautiful, just beautiful," murmured Julia, finishing her shoot and sinking to the soft grassy mat of green velvet, her arms flung over her head.

"Yes, I agree." Brad said softly, his tone conveying a different meaning to his words as he stood looking down at her.

Julia raised her eyes to look at Brad and was caught by his compelling gaze. His touch on her bare shoulder as he lowered himself beside her sent her heart racing. On one bended knee he watched her while gently sliding his fingers to the well of her throat, then to her lips where his thumb slowly traced the outline of her mouth.

With a small moan, she parted her lips as Brad dropped down beside her, his mouth covering hers. His kiss was slow, yet deliberate. She felt his tongue searching hungrily for hers. Impatiently, she moved her tongue wantonly until it became the searcher, greedily exploring the recesses of his mouth.

With the barest hesitation, Brad looked at Julia with lifted brow. He stared at her parted lips, her heaving breast, and with a groan, lay down beside her, enfolding her in his arms and crushing her to his chest.

Julia's body was aflame as Brad's taut form touched her. Once again his tongue sought hers. Her lips were warm and moist. His hands began to trace the outline of her soft tender curves, moving languidly from her throat to her breasts, brushing her taut nipple, then gliding down to her smooth thighs. Her flesh tingled at his touch. She twisted her body to feel more of him, wrapping her arms tightly around his neck. Julia thought, At last the picture has come to life. He is real and more than I imagined. She felt as though she were drowning, then flying high into the sky. Her emotions soared at these new and delightful sensations. Soared as high as the birds that suddenly began calling to one another. The high-pitched sound invaded Julia's senses. Pushing her hands against Brad's chest, she sat up. "Brad, what are we doing? I'm sorry—Samantha—I—I—I don't know."

"Don't know what, Julia?" asked Brad. "What?" he repeated, standing up. "Don't know that your body responded to mine like it was supposed to, that your lips wanted mine? There's an attraction here, lady, that neither of us can deny. We felt it yesterday and we're feeling it now. Tell me, Julia, what is it that you don't know?" Brad finished harshly, his black eyes smoldering.

"You know quite well what I mean," sputtered Julia, brushing his reaching hand away as she stood up, gathering her camera in an attempt to appear calm. "You know that you, that Sam . . . oh, forget it," Julia said as she started down the hill to the car. "Sam's waiting for us."

Julia all but tumbled down the hill in her mad haste to put distance between them. Her thoughts were reeling, her flesh still tingling from his touch. She shuddered even as the sun heated her bare shoulders. Her heart pounded heavily as she recalled Brad's stinging words of truth. She knew he was attracted to her. From the beginning he had openly admired her, and now, he obviously felt her own attraction to him, feelings she tried to hide. She had been unsuccessful. The raw emotion she'd just exhibited at the top of the hill confused and frightened her. What if he realizes that for months I've held the image of him in my mind while all the time I was falling in love? What if he guesses how close to the truth he is? Julia had reached the car. She leaned forward, resting her body to support her shaking legs before she opened the door and climbed inside. Sitting back, leaning her head on the cushioned headrest, eyes closed, she waited for Brad.

Brad stood motionless watching Julia hurry down the hill, his ebony eyes filled with anger. Beautiful women, more games, he thought, watching as Julia shivered, rubbing her arms as she stumbled to the car. When she rested her head, Brad's eyes narrowed. Crying? he thought with a wry smile.

Slowly he descended the hill, never taking his eyes off Julia, watching her as she sat silently, not moving. What is going on in that beautiful head? Brad mused. Much as I hate to admit it, she intrigues me. She's different. Judging from what happened on this hill just now, I'm not unattractive to her. She showed desire. And now she's trying to hide her fears and tears from me. Why? Brad's eyes softened as he reached the passenger side of the car. Julia sat unmoving, eyes closed.

Julia felt Brad watching her. Slowly she opened her eyes, gazing up at him. His eyes no longer blazed at her; they were full of questions, but he did not speak. They stared at one another for a long moment before Julia quietly repeated, "Sam's waiting for us."

Hearing her soft voice and losing himself in the depths of those sad, dark eyes, Brad was jolted with the realization that he wanted this woman—and not as a passing interlude. For years since

Laura's death Brad had avoided commitment to one woman. He'd learned how to play the bachelor game exceptionally well, but here he was, yearning to possess a woman he had known for one day.

After a long moment Brad walked around the car, easily sliding behind the steering wheel. As he started the engine, he looked at Julia long and hard. A smile played against his mouth, lingered, then ran up to his eyes. His lips parted in a devilish grin as he moved the car slowly onto the road. They drove the rest of the way in silence, broken only by Julia's directions.

"Oh, here you guys are," shouted Samantha, waving from the pool. "What took you so long?" she asked breathlessly, as she toweled her dripping hair. "Brad," she rushed on, "come meet some folks. I've bent their ears out of shape bragging about you." As Samantha pulled Brad toward a cluster of sunbathers, Julia went in search of her cousin Caroline, stopping along the way to greet some of the same family members and friends from yesterday's picnic.

"Julia, I'd just about given up on you. I called Frieda. She said you should have been here. Where's Brad?" her cousin said all in one breath, pulling Julia up the porch steps and into the dining room. The table was laden with rows of steaming chafing dishes filled with delicious smelling foods of all kinds. As the aroma reached Julia's nose and her stomach growled loudly, she remembered that she'd had only a cup of coffee with her mother and Brad and that seemed like ages ago. "Mmmm, Caro," Julia said. Stuffing hot hash brown potatoes into her mouth, she continued putting some of everything on her plate, including two hot buttered biscuits; "delicious. . . and I knew you just *had* to have these biscuits. If you hadn't. . ." Julia finished in a threatening tone.

The walnut-brown woman beside her laughed, her merry brown eyes twinkling. Though cousins, Caroline was fifteen years older than Julia. At forty-three she'd never married. An executive vice-president of an insurance firm, she was successful enough to have purchased her own home and several other properties in the city. She was buxom, her body more round than voluptuous. Her face was plain, but one forgot the lack of beauty when she smiled, for it reached her eyes, triggering points of warm light.

She was a good cook and no one ever passed through town

without making a stop at Cousin Caroline's to eat.

"I swear, Julia," Caroline said in her mellow voice, "I still don't know where you put all of that food. Two biscuits! Look at you. Not an extra ounce of fat anywhere." She groaned, playfully pinching Julia's midriff. "Everything I eat sits and sits and sits," she finished, as they both burst into laughter, walking outside to join the crowd at the spacious swimming pool.

"Where is he?" Caroline asked, her gaze scanning the crowd as Julia sat at an umbrella table, seeking the shade with relief.

"Just follow the bikinis," Julia said, nodding her head toward a cluster of young, slender bodies gleaming with sun-tan oil. "He's there in the center. Can't you see?" she finished, stabbing a piece of potato and poking it into her mouth.

"Hmmm. Yes, I do see," her cousin said with eyebrow arched as she walked towards Brad and Samantha, turning once to glance quizzically at Julia. Julia missed the look for she was suddenly pounced upon by the twins and other chattering little people, some of the boys making mock muscle-man poses.

"All right, all right, little hams, I get the picture," quipped Julia, as she stood up. "Let's go get the camera." Lost in a sea of small pushing and shoving bodies, Julia failed to see Brad's look as he watched her leave, his dark eyes unfathomable.

With a start, Julia awoke. She shivered, rubbing the goose bumps on her arms. She looked around and found herself on the screened-in patio where earlier she had sought refuge. After shooting pictures, swimming, eating again and gossiping with the relatives, Julia had looked for and found a quiet corner where she promptly dozed off. Now she squinted at the sky, wondering what time it was and why it was so quiet; then she remembered that everyone probably had gone to get ready for the moonlight cruise. Wondering if Brad and Sam had left her here, she thought back to a few hours ago, remembering Brad's touch, and she shivered again.

"It's much warmer around front. There's still a little sun." Startled, Julia looked up to see Brad leaning against the door, watching her. His serious ebony eyes held a question which was put into words when he extended his hand, saying, "Friends?"

Julia responded by holding out her hand, smiling warmly.

"Friends," she replied.

"Good," Brad said softly, holding her hand tightly and easily pulling her to her feet. As Julia stood up, the lounge chair she had been resting on tilted. She stumbled, but was pulled lightly to Brad's chest. The feel of her breasts against him sent shock waves through Julia's body. Pulse pounding, she released herself.

As they walked down the patio steps and started toward the front of the house where the sun still shone weakly, her thoughts were a jumble of confusion. Something's happening to me. First I can't stand the man, then I want him to touch me. When he does, I don't want him to stop—then, I hate him for touching me—.

"Julia," Brad's voice broke the silence.

"Ummm," she murmured.

"Where are you?"

"What?"

"I know you're here walking beside me, but I can't help feeling you're really very far away. Can I help?" Brad asked, his expression serious.

Julia couldn't tell him that he was the problem, not the solution. All day, no matter what activity she was involved in, romping with the younger group, rocking a toddler to sleep or swimming, she'd felt his gaze upon her. When their eyes met, his were unreadable. At times, his scrutiny was so intense some relatives noticed, grinned at Julia, and continued their conversation.

Once, when Julia had quieted the sobs and wiped the tears of an eleven-year-old cousin who'd fallen and badly scraped her knees, she found Brad watching them, his eyes burning intently as he looked at the child. He had turned abruptly away, but not before Julia had seen the brief flash of pain and torment shadow his face.

"No, Brad," she finally answered him. They were seated at a bistro table, one of many dotting the expansive front lawn. "I'm fine," Julia continued, speaking softly. "I'll work things out like I usually do. My mother always told me, if nothing else, I've got stick-to-it-iveness."

Brad's face broke into a broad grin. "I'm afraid your mother is wrong, definitely wrong," he emphasized, his lingering gaze touching her mouth, her neck, her breasts, even her crossed legs, before they settled on her puzzled dark eyes. "No, that's not *all* you've got," Brad said with a chuckle that started deep in his throat and burst through his grin. His laugh was infectious and Julia laughed with him, somehow not embarrassed by his blatant flirtatious appraisal of her.

"You ought to do that more often," Julia said.

"You, too. I haven't heard you laugh since first we met in your mother's kitchen."

Julia smiled, feeling relaxed in Brad's presence for the first time.

He reached over, gently cupping her chin, his thumb slowly tracing the outline of her jaw. "Why couldn't we have done this yesterday?" he asked, his voice sounding curiously far away, as he removed his hand and sat back in his chair.

"You mean sit here talking like civilized people?" Julia tried to be flip but found it increasingly hard to concentrate. Her skin had gotten hot again.

"Julia," his voice, quiet yet determined, "my offer to help if I can still stands."

Julia looked at Brad, assailed by a terrible sense of frustration as the tenderness in his voice shook her to the core. Brad. She wanted to whisper his name and brush his lips with hers. Instead, her voice growing husky, she finally spoke, "When I was driving from the airport yesterday, all I could think of was 'Brad' from Paris, and what did he mean to our Sam? Attending a backyard barbecue just to indulge the whims of a homesick young woman didn't sit too well with me."

Brad looked amused. "So you came to check out the mysterious man yourself," he said dryly.

Julia continued as if Brad hadn't spoken. "If I thought for the barest fraction of a second you were toying with Sam, you would have to take on big sister Julia." She flushed when Brad tilted his head, a small smile playing about his mouth as he intentionally misconstrued her meaning.

Julia continued, "Sam appears happier than I thought she would be. I see that you respect her and she likes you. My parents like you. You've stolen the hearts of all my female relatives, young and old." Julia finished with a shrug. Answering the question in Brad's eyes, she said, "Yes, I like you too, Brad." No, Julia thought,

I've fallen in love with you, Brad. She stood up. "Let's go find Sam. We'd better get moving if we're to make the boat tonight."

Brad stood, watching Julia hurry into the house in search of Samantha. His face went through a series of expressions from puzzlement to dark anguish, to stark disbelief until finally with realization, a broad smile engulfed his handsome features, lighting up his dancing dark eyes. Walking lightly, he followed Julia into the house.

Chapter III

"You're stunning, Ju," Samantha said. The sisters stood side by side looking in the oversize mirror in Julia's bedroom.

"Thanks, Sam. You're gorgeous as usual. But does one expect anything less from Paris's darling Sammí?" teased Julia. Their reflections complemented one another. Julia's white silk *crepe de chine* skirt fell in a soft swirl around her ankles. Over it she wore a white tunic length sweater of soft pure silk with a cable-edged ballet neckline. Her only jewelry was long golden earrings, the perfect foil to her short cap of hair. Gold-toned sandals completed her outfit.

Samantha was simple elegance in a short tangerine silk tank dress with scooped neck, caught at the waist with gold chain links.

"Aw, shucks, the Hart girls just got' em beat, that's all," drawled Samantha, slapping her thigh and stamping her foot before breaking out in a fit of laughter.

Turning serious, Samantha threw an arm around Julia's shoulders and gave her a quick squeeze before sitting down on the bed. "I'm glad we talked this afternoon, Julia. All the letters that flew across the ocean—you never mentioned your desire to own your own photo art gallery! But what about becoming senior associate art director at the magazine? Did your boss change his mind about retiring? I know you wanted that job badly."

"Oh, of course I want it. Very much. The gallery is a long way down the road. Only a dream right now." Julia was staring into space and didn't see the quirk of Samantha's eyebrow as she filed away a mental note. "The promotion is mine," continued Julia. "Jim Anderson is champing at the bit waiting for me to fall on my face. We both went after that job. I won. I'm not about to give it up for a dream."

"Jim? You've mentioned him quite a bit these past few months. Something to share?" teased Samantha.

"No, not really," Julia answered. "We work well together. We've become good friends again since he got over his disappointment in not getting the job."

"Become?"

"Yes, smarty pants. Become. And yes, he's tried to be more than just friends, but . . ."

"You still have that old Ralph Manning hurt, don't you, Ju?" Samantha said softly. "Hasn't there been anyone that's mattered since college?"

Julia's expression clouded in bitter memory. Ralph Manning. Like bile, his name caught in her throat, waiting to be released in a cry of disgust. Old hurt, she thought. No, an ever present hurt. Because of you the man I'm falling in love with can never be mine. Unlike Ralph Manning, my dearest friend, my sister Sam, I could never betray you. Dispelling the sudden feeling of gloom, Julia shrugged her shoulders, giving Samantha a bright smile, "Silly sis, I'm not living in the Cloisters. I've had friends, but . . . it's just that I've never met anyone I've wanted to be with . . . after . . ." Julia's voice ended weakly.

Julia and Samantha had talked non-stop while preparing for the cruise. Samantha's teasing questions were about Julia's love life, while Julia had asked question after question about Brad.

Samantha was surprised to learn that Julia had no idea Brad was *the* Bradford Coleman, successful restaurant entrepreneur and owner of the fast-food franchises. "But Ju, I thought I told you. Long ago!" exclaimed Samantha.

Indignant, Julia said she wasn't into reading the business pages on a daily basis and had no idea this "Brad" existed except from Samantha's letters. "You neglected to give a last name, Sammí," clipped Julia, using the French pronunciation. "It was always Brad, Brad, Brad," Julia said pointedly.

As Samantha proceeded to relate the story of Brad's involvement in a New York restaurant scandal several years ago, Julia vaguely began to recall the incident. Brad's businesses and reputation were in jeopardy as the result of a woman patron suing the corporation for false advertising. She claimed to have been near death after consuming meat prepared with peanut oil, which when ingested by her caused a deadly allergic reaction. The woman contended that the store's 'list of ingredients' boldly proclaimed, "NO PEANUT OIL." The print and video media were sensationalizing the trial. Special interest groups formed overnight protesting anything and everything about fast food stores, from the unhealthy salad bars to the pollution-causing styrofoam. Brad was exonerated; his attorneys proved that his ex-partner Charlie Pierce had deliberately set out to ruin Brad.

So that's why he looked familiar to me when I first saw him, Julia thought, recalling flashes of blurry newspaper photos and the TV evening news showing Brad hurrying down the court building steps. She also remembered the tabloids referring to him as the "elusive bachelor."

"I'm worried about him." Samantha's voice intruded upon Julia's reverie, her somber tone immediately catching and holding her sister's attention. Samantha continued, Julia listening intently, "When he called me at my apartment to tell me an emergency had arisen, that he was leaving Paris immediately, I became frightened. I'd never heard such anger in his voice. Anger, and . . . something else I couldn't quite detect then. But now, I think I know. It was—despair. I recognize it now."

"How?" Julia asked quietly.

"I heard it again, the day he arrived here from New York. He received a phone call. I answered. It was a woman. The same voice I heard when she'd called an hour before Brad pulled into the driveway. She sounded . . . not annoyed, but . . . worried."

"Worried?"

"Yes. Like she was trying hard to sound calm. But the strain came through anyway."

"But how did you hear Brad?" Julia persisted.

"When I handed him the phone he started speaking before I left the room," Samantha replied, shrugging her shoulders. "When he heard the woman's voice he asked, 'What happened?' He listened, then he shouted, 'What?' He yelled so furiously I thought I'd heard a clap of thunder. So I didn't walk away, Julia. I stayed outside listening." Samantha had the good sense to look embarrassed at Julia's stern look. Samantha continued. "He began barking orders so rapidly I only caught snatches—he mentioned his attorney, and a name, something like Pierce. I couldn't hear all of it. Then he was silent. The woman talked for a long time. I looked into the room but his back was to me. Julia," Samantha said in a small voice, "I think if I could've seen his face I would've seen tears in his eyes. His head was in the palm of one hand, while the other gripped the phone. His shoulders were slumped. Then he spoke, Julia. The sound brought tears to my eyes. All I could hear, because his voice had dropped, was, 'Why? Why now? This cannot happen to me again. Not now. Not now.' Julia, that hoarse whisper . . . so full of pain . . ." Samantha's own voice ended in a whisper.

"What happened? Did he find you listening?"

"No. Before he hung up he said, 'No. I won't be traveling to D.C. with her. I'm coming back.' That's when I hurried away," Samantha ended. After a moment she went on.

"When he came looking for me, his face showed nothing, but there was no light in his eyes. He told me a change of plans was necessary and that he must return to New York on Monday. He apologized about the trip to D.C. He said, 'You'll still have your sister's company.'"

Julia was silent for a long moment, trying to make sense of what she'd just heard.

When she and Sam had talked long-distance about the upcoming reunion Sam had informed Julia about a little 'side trip' to D.C. that she had planned. "Just the three of us," Sam had said, "you, me and my friend Brad." No matter how much Julia protested, Samantha would not budge. She insisted that Julia be a part of her "surprise." "You'll find out about it in D.C.," she had said. Julia had smiled at her sister's barely-contained excitement that fairly crackled over the telephone wire. She finally agreed, to Samantha's delight.

Knowing her willful sister would not divulge the secret until they were in D.C., she had put the matter out of her mind.

"Yes, of course I'm going with you to D.C.," Julia responded to Samantha's persistent questioning. "We just won't be a threesome, that's all." Thank God for that, Julia thought. She'd been wondering how to tell Sam she had changed her mind. After meeting Brad, there was no way she could have accompanied them to Washington as previously planned. Now, though perplexed and a little sad at Brad's sudden emergency, she was relieved that he was leaving.

Samantha, curious about Julia's obvious relief at Brad's sudden change of plans, teased, "You're mighty relieved that Brad's not coming with us. Not trying to avoid my friend are you? Come on, share now."

"Share. Look who's talking about share. Making me wait nearly a week before you'll share your mysterious secret," Julia said, playfully pinching Samantha's arm. "And in D.C. too. You're not going to turn out to be a CIA agent, are you?"

Samantha's eyes twinkled. "Ju, you're going to be so proud of me," she said.

"I'm already proud of you . . ." Julia broke off as Frieda Hart's voice floated up the stairs.

"Girls, what are you doing up there? The boat's going to pull out without half the Hart family."

Julia inhaled deeply, coughing as her nostrils filled with whiffs of honeysuckle, jasmine and brine. Every table on the top deck of the replica of a nineteenth-century paddle wheeler held a bowl of perfumed blossoms while garlands decorated every available pole. She was leaning her elbows on the boat railing, hugging her arms, as she gazed at harbor lights shining on the murkiness of the Elizabeth River. A smile played against her mouth as her thoughts turned to the events of the evening, which was nearing an end, the boat heading downriver to its berth. The band was playing soft music and the family chatter and gaiety had quieted to a conversational din. Young lovers had found shadowy corners while some of the younger set were dozing in adult laps or had found table space to rest their sleepy heads.

She thought about Brad. At dinner she had been seated across the table from him as he sat between her mother and Sam. As he charmed all the females at the table with his wit and Paris society stories, his eyes would capture and hold Julia's for long moments. When he had spoken to her she was able to reply in normal tones, carrying her part of the conversation with ease and sophistication. Once she had caught a look that passed between Brad and Samantha. Sam had spoken softly, Brad nodded, replying only with a tender look. Before she could turn away, Brad caught her stare and smiled at her. Frieda spoke to him and he turned to answer, but not before Julia saw the smile light up his eyes. For a moment, Julia's thoughts became confused but she quickly shook off impending doubts. She was enjoying the evening, including being in Brad's presence. She refused to allow her jumbled feelings to intrude. She had pushed them beneath the surface.

Now, as she hugged herself, she shivered, her hands flying up to catch a sneeze.

"Catching cold?" asked Brad softly, handing her his handkerchief.

"It's the flowers. Thank you," she said, handing back the large blue square of cotton. Julia was not startled; she actually anticipated his seeking her out. Having decided to enjoy these last hours with the intriguing Brad Coleman, she even looked forward to sitting across from him at the breakfast table in the morning before he drove back to New York. In her heart, she knew that she would never cheat on her sister with Brad, so she would allow these moments with him to be pleasant ones. She looked up at Brad's face to find him watching her questioningly.

"What's happened to you?" he said softly. "Is it the night air, the honeysuckle or old riverboats," he continued, laughing gently at her bemused look.

"What do you mean?" Julia asked. "I'm enjoying all three, but I detect something else in your question," replied Julia with a smile in her voice.

"Samantha said nothing ever slips by you. She's right."

At the mention of Samantha's name, Julia's smile disappeared and her eyes clouded over only for the barest moment, yet Brad noticed. Puzzled, he continued, for the smile had returned to Julia's lips and eyes.

"I mean you have detected correctly," Brad explained. "You appear to have made a decision to charm the pants off me tonight. You're playing your part superbly. I'm charmed," Brad ended in a soft whisper.

The deep timbre of his voice, even in a whisper caused tremors to ripple in Julia's stomach. He was so close their shoulders touched with every swell of the boat.

Julia felt warmed all over, the flush lingering to tingle her cheeks.

"Ummm . . . and what else has our Sam been telling you? Should I worry that our family skeletons have been let loose?" Julia asked lightly, wishing he could know her "act" was real.

"Not so much the *family's* skeletons as . . ." Brad's teasing voice trailed to a halt. He threw back his head and laughed at the astonishment on Julia's face.

Brad was enjoying himself. Since his earlier understanding of the cause of Julia's reluctance toward him, he ached to erase those errant thoughts from her mind. The idea of him and Samantha as lovers amused him, but where in hell did she get the idea in the first place? he wondered. With all those hours of "catch-up" talk, as Frieda had called it, what in the world were they discussing not to have gotten around to his and Samantha's relationship, that they were only *friends*? But no matter, I'll take care of that tonight, thought Brad. All evening he'd watched Julia and he knew that she watched him. Each was so aware of the other it was a wonder that the volatility of their vibes did not reverberate through every person separating them. At the long-unused stirrings in his heart, Brad had felt light-headed, turning on a charm of his own. When he had seen Julia standing at the rail of the boat, the warm night wind lifting the short ringlets of hair, allowing them to fall back in disarray, he had wanted to hug her to his chest and let his fingers comb the cluster of unruly curls.

Now here he was laughing and teasing her. I haven't acted this way with a woman since Laura and my children died, Brad thought. The memory of his dead wife darkened his eyes with pain and anger. The anguish and fear of falling in love with another beautiful woman gripped his heart, but his fears were soon dispelled. Julia was not Laura, he reminded himself. I want this woman and I'm not returning to New York until she knows it. With that, he turned to answer Julia's questioning look.

"About those skeletons," he began. "Picture yourself in a foreign country surrounded by false friends and plastic fortune hunters. What would you do if one day you found a fellow-American, a real friend who is likeable, an eligible bachelor, a good listener, a very good listener," Brad emphasized, "who listens to all the stories about the family back in America. Especially the ones about big sister Julia?" Brad answered his own question, "You'd naturally want your family to meet this wonderful friend. What better occasion than the family reunion?"

Julia, matching Brad's playful mood, returned, "Ummm–I think I'd do exactly the same thing, and I'd make sure big sister Julia is informed of everything that was said about her, everything," concluded Julia, nodding vigorously.

"Everything?"

"Everything. Now where would you like to begin?"

"Early morning sunrises. Especially the one after Zeus was killed."

Julia's eyes widened in surprise. "Zeus. But that was so long ago."

"Samantha was eleven. You were fifteen."

"Zeus," Julia repeated, remembering their pet collie, struck and killed by a car. "Zeus and sunrises," Julia said softly. "When Zeus was killed, we both cried ourselves to sleep that night. When I awakened, it was early, nearly dawn. I'd left my bedroom to watch the sunrise from the back porch, as I often did. Sam finally found me. We watched the sunrise together, a first for Sam. She was awed. After that, we'd sometimes find one another on the back porch watching the sun come up." Julia looked at Brad. "Sam has never talked to me about it."

Brad, not looking at Julia, but staring across the dark water said, "She never forgot it."

Recalling the many times spent in a Paris cafe or in his restaurant when she would wander in, hoping he would be there, Samantha would talk wistfully of her friends left behind so long ago in America. She talked to him about her hopes and dreams, and her life long after the name Sammi would be a faded memory. She had spoken about her family and always of her big sister Julia. Brad had never minded the pretty young model's incessant talk. He sensed her need and had come to look upon her as the sister he never had. An only child, he had missed taunts and bickering between brother and sister that was a constant bane to his boyhood friends. Through Samantha, he was experiencing a side of his personality that heretofore had been unexposed. The world he lived in demanded and expected no less than his well-established, austere, authoritative approach to people and business.

He liked the banter, the give-and-take, between him and Samantha, neither of them asking more of the other than they were willing to share. For all her youth, Samantha was keenly alert to the needs of others. She was wise, sophisticated and had her feet planted solidly on the ground. He had come to look forward to their meetings because he knew that before long, Samantha would mention the latest letter or call from Julia. More and more he wondered about this woman back in the States who so obviously loved the sister who in turn spoke glowingly about her. He thought about the girl who in so grown-up a fashion, had eased the fears of a youngster's first encounter with death. Now Samantha, always an avid people lover, after being so successful a career woman, was about to embark on her detoured journey: the study of cultural anthropology. Her decision, a secret she'd kept from everyone but her parents and Brad, was long in the planning. Samantha planned to surprise Julia once they were in D.C., where Samantha was to finalize her acceptance into Georgetown University.

Brad, turning to Julia, spoke softly, his tender gaze drinking in her loveliness. He repeated, "No, she never forgot that night. She told me how she had watched the coming of dawn; how the red-gold ball hovered on the horizon. You told her that she'd witnessed the birth of a new day and to think of Zeus as beginning his after-life that very moment and not to be sad for him. You said for her to be sad for us because *we* are left behind to bear the hurt, *we* are the deprived ones."

Julia, husky-voiced, whispered, "You make that day seem as though it were yesterday." After a moment, in an attempt to recover the lightness of their mood, she said, "And what other skeletons has our Sam dug up for you?" Her voice wavered a little, uncertain as to how much Brad knew about her.

Gasping, the warmth disappearing from her tawny cheeks, the harbor lights shimmering on her pale reflection, a bitter memory ripped through her. Ralph Manning! No. Sam wouldn't.

Brad watched the array of emotions play over Julia's face. Suddenly, as if by some pre-arranged signal, the animation left her face. Her dark eyes dulled with dismay, the lashes dropping to hide her inner pain.

Though confused by her sharp change of mood, Brad felt such tenderness for her that he wanted to ease whatever pain she was experiencing. In one fluid motion, he turned her to him, embracing her tightly, his chin resting on her dark curls. He breathed in the sweet scent of her hair as stray ringlets tickled his nose. Slowly, he caressed her shoulders and the nape of her neck until the tightness in her shoulders eased. As she relaxed, Brad tenderly stroked Julia's forehead. Gradually the frown left her brow; her clenched jaw loosened. Julia put both arms around Brad's waist, her head resting against his chest.

For a long moment she stayed, feeling secure in his arms and annoyed with herself for allowing her foolish thoughts to invade their peaceful time together. She sighed, starting to release him, thinking that Samantha was one lucky woman, when suddenly she stiffened and with lightening speed, jerked herself from Brad's embrace. Hands on his chest, she pushed him away from her. Julia's flesh had turned cold, her body shook and her eyes shimmered with tears of rage. Backing away from him, she whispered in a halting, unrecognizable voice.

"Don't . . . ever . . . do . . . that again . . . Don't ever . . . touch . . . me again." She stumbled away, disappearing down the stairs to the bottom deck of the boat.

Brad stood as if struck by a lightening bolt, his mind racing back to what he'd done to cause such a vehement outburst. Coming up with no answer, he leaned on the boat railing, staring into nothingness, his eyes dark and troubled. He had no time to assess the last few moments because the boat was docking.

When at last he reached the main deck, he scanned the crowd, searching for Julia. He finally saw her. One of the first in line to leave the boat as soon as the ramp was in place, she was still distraught. From a distance, Brad could see the strain on her face as she halfheartedly engaged in conversation with several talkative cousins, all loudly agreeing that this year's reunion committee had done a splendid job. Brad did not try to reach her as she ran down the ramp. Somehow he knew she would only withdraw from him; but he was determined to get to the bottom of her actions. Something had frightened her out of her wits.

When Brad reached his car in the parking lot, he found Samantha waiting for him, sitting atop the hood, swinging her crossed shapely ankles. He wasn't surprised; he'd driven her and Julia to the dock. And neither did Julia's absence surprise him.

Samantha hopped down as he approached. Expecting to see the usual bright smile on her pretty face, Brad was amazed at the somber look in her eyes and no smile at all. Not speaking, he opened the door for her and she climbed in, sitting silently as he began easing the car through the crowd of stragglers walking to their cars. Following the same route he had taken, Brad drove toward the Hart home. During the silent drive, Brad assumed that Samantha's mood was centered around Julia.

It's uncanny, he mused. He realized they were close but they acted more like twins than sisters four years apart, they were so attuned to one another. Brad waited. He knew the exuberant Samantha could not remain silent for long when another human was in hearing distance. He did not have to wait long. Samantha turned to him asking, but without accusation, "What went wrong? What did you do to her?" At Brad's quick glance at her, Samantha repeated, "What did you do? The last time I looked you two were doing great, talking, smiling at one another . . . even *laughing*." Samantha smiled at the look of amazement that suddenly covered Brad's handsome features. His eyes filled with questions. Still smiling, Samantha continued.

"Why do you think you two had that whole shadowy deck area to yourselves for so long without other couples joining you or the kids wanting to pester Julia?" Samantha's grin widened as she chuckled at the thought. "When M'Dear and Cousin Caro saw you join Julia, they stationed themselves at opposite ends of the deck, steering traffic in another direction. You two noticed nothing but one another."

Brad finally smiled. "That obvious, huh?"

"Obvious! A person would have to be a newborn babe not to have noticed what was happening to the two of you tonight. You weren't the problem, we decided. It was Julia. She was the one practicing avoidance."

"We decided?" Brad echoed.

"Oh, Brad. You were given the once-over by the aunts and uncles yesterday and approval today at Cousin Caro's," Samantha scoffed. "Everyone was aware of the attraction between you two. What I want to know is, what happened? The last time I looked, Julia was in your arms. I looked again and she was running down the stairs. She looked scared," Samantha ended, with a stern glance at Brad.

Brad scarcely heard Samantha after her remark about his and Julia's attraction to one another. So, he thought with a wry smile, the electricity had not gone unnoticed. He shook his head in amazement at the relatives. They've got us as a twosome already; he grinned at the pleasant thought rolling around in his head. In answer to Samantha's questions, he said, "I don't know. One minute she was resting her head on my chest, the next she acted as if I was attacking her. She cried for me not to ever touch her again."

Samantha, hearing the anguish in Brad's voice, turned quietly to him. "Tell me exactly what you did."

Brad, bewildered, but noting the sudden alarm in Samantha's voice, went on. "I was trying to soothe her. I hugged her, brushed her face with my fingers, massaged the tension from her shoulders and neck. She had just begun to relax when I ran my fingers through her hair–"

Brad felt Samantha stiffen beside him. Her soft gasp caused him to pull into the lot of an all-night diner. Stopping the car, he got out, saying, "Let's talk."

Grabbing her hand, his long-legged stride quickly bringing

them to the entrance and up the steps, he guided her to a booth, giving an order to the waitress on the way.

Brad waited until the waitress returned with two tall glasses of iced tea, then leaned back in the booth, slowly sipping the tea, never taking his eyes from Samantha's face. Setting the glass on the table but still gripping it, he waited.

"Brad," Samantha began, "Julia will never forgive me if she finds out I told you." She hesitated, then stated, "You love her." Brad said nothing, his eyes veiled.

Samantha sighed, took a sip of the cool drink and settled back in the booth. "M'Dear always called Julia a born leader who loved the world and the world loved her back. From nursery school on she was the brightest and the bossiest, yet her happy and trusting nature won over the toughest school bully. M'Dear never let her out of sight whenever we went to the malls because Julia would think nothing of starting conversations with strangers, ending up inviting them home for dinner."

Brad's eyes softened. He recalled that the first time he saw her. The natural friendliness and love she and her family had exhibited toward one another was obvious.

Samantha was saying, "As she grew older, we all teased her about her collection . . . her collection of friends." She paused. "I believe she started with me," she said softly. "When Julia left for college she didn't change. She just started collecting in the District of Columbia. She was happy, so M'Dear and Dad relaxed, realizing Julia would always be Julia. She was excelling in her studies, so what more should they ask?" Samantha shrugged, spreading her hands in a hopeless gesture.

"But," Samantha went on, "in her senior year at Howard, something happened to her. Three weeks after returning from the Christmas break, she was home saying she wasn't going back. M'Dear and Dad could take that in stride. However, they were not prepared for how she looked." Samantha stopped. Brad's brooding dark eyes watched her intently. Samantha whispered, "She'd cut off all her hair." Noting Brad's eyes flicker with surprise, she said, "You saw the family photos in the living room. Julia with a mop of hair?"

Recalling the pictures he'd seen on the walls and tables of two skinny little girls at various ages, both with long dark curls, Brad nodded. Tilting his head, he looked at Samantha's closely-cropped hair that was her model's trademark.

"I cut mine by choice," Samantha replied to his silent question.

His voice harsh, Brad questioned, "What happened to her?"

"She lost the love and trust of a friend and it devastated her. No, not a man," Samantha said in answer to Brad's raised brow. "Sunny Peterson, her roommate and buddy since they started school together. Sunny never returned after the break. After two days Julia called her home. Sunny's mother informed Julia that Sunny was in the hospital and was comatose after having an abortion that had gone wrong.

"And Sunny's mother hysterically accused Julia of being selfish and self-centered, too busy being *Miss Popularity* to care about a friend who'd asked for her help." Samantha paused as the waitress who had noticed Brad's signal replaced their drinks. "Mrs. Peterson's accusations," Samantha continued, "stunned Julia. Because she realized they were true. She remembered being stopped by Sunny in halls, the library, the cafeteria where Sunny would say half- jokingly, 'Partner, I need to borrow some of your gray matter. You've put me on the shelf.' Busy with her own hectic schedule of research papers, exams and campus activities, Julia never took the time to ask, 'Can I help?' That's when Julia thought about the abortion and Ralph Manning, Sunny's boyfriend. Ralph was the classic womanizer and one of the few people Julia had given a wide berth. He sensed her dislike of him. His arrogance made him more determined to pursue 'Queen Julia' as he had called her and his advances increased."

Samantha stopped as she looked at Brad's narrowed eyes. "No," she said, holding up a hand as if to squash the thought that was beginning to invade Brad's senses. "Julia made it a point never to be caught alone with him," Samantha said, feeling Brad relax. "Ralph was a toucher, a horrible habit that he thought adoring females loved, but it always repulsed Julia.

"When in conversation with a woman he would possessively run his fingers through her hair. No one escaped. Short hair? He'd twirl his fingers through the ringlets. Natural styles? He'd trace the outline of the sideburns. Revolted, Julia would slap his hand away whenever he caught her unaware."

Brad, with a start, began to realize the bitter memory his actions on the deck had stirred up in Julia.

Samantha continued. "The day Julia learned about Sunny, friends came by to be with her. Ralph Manning was in the group. When he caught her alone, he whispered, 'Stop the act. Your one excuse is gone now.' He started kissing her, raking his hands through her hair. Finally she bit his lips to stop him. He tried to back away but his ring had gotten tangled in her hair. Julia started screaming in panic as she pushed and slapped at him. Her friends threw Ralph out, but couldn't calm Julia. She kept screaming, 'She's dying! My friend . . .my friend . . .I'm sorry . . . sorry . . .' Frightened, they drove her to the hospital where she stayed the night, sedated."

Samantha paused, recalling the tears she'd shed when Julia had told her the story years later. At Brad's nod, she continued. "Back home the next day, the vision in her mirror showed her struggling with Ralph, his hand tangled in her hair. She took the scissors and cut it all off. She keeps it cut," Samantha finished, sitting quietly, feeling Julia's pain.

"What happened to Sunny?"

"She came out of the coma after three weeks, but she can never have children. She never returned to school," Samantha paused, a frown puckering her brow. "Funny, they were so close, but Sunny never returned Julia's calls or answered her letters. Mrs. Peterson always answered the phone saying that Sunny was resting or out or said that she'd given Sunny Julia's message. Finally, Julia stopped calling and writing, believing Sunny was too bitter to continue their friendship."

"And Julia?" Brad asked.

"After staying under the wing of Cousin Caro for awhile, Julia became a new person. Returning to school, she graduated as valedictorian."

"Caro?"

"Yes, Caro," she insisted. "You've seen her," Samantha smiled. "She was born strong and aggressive. She and Julia have always been close. Cousin Caroline realized that if Julia was to bounce back quickly from her malaise, she'd do it in record time without the babying of her parents."

Brad stirred when Samantha tapped his hand. He looked at her, his mind racing back to his last moments with Julia. Thoughtfully, he rose, placed some bills on the table and guided Samantha to the car. Neither spoke during the drive home.

At the sound of the car door closing, footsteps, and whispered goodnights, Julia closed her eyes. Since the silent drive home with her parents from the dock, she'd sat quietly on the front porch steps, waiting for Brad's car. She realized her behavior must have confused and alienated him, and she wanted to apologize. She did not want his one last image of her to be that of a hysterical woman.

But after an hour, it became apparent that Brad and Samantha had driven elsewhere. As she lay in bed, the sounds of night were intruded upon by the purring of a car's engine coming to a stop. When Samantha opened the door to their bedroom, Julia, feigning sleep, did not stir. She did not want to talk to Sam.

Chapter IV

Bells . . . the repeated chime of bells finally intruded into Brad's drugged sleep. Flinging an arm to the nightstand he silenced the radio clock alarm. More bells. The persistent jangle of the telephone bell. Stretching, he reached for the phone and lifted the receiver. "Hello," he mumbled, his voice thick with sleep.

"Mr. Coleman? Are you aware that your latest victim is near death? Whose fault is it this time? Mr. Coleman?"

"What? Who is this?"

"Kate Hawley. *Daily News*. Is it true . . .?"

The reporter's voice was lost in the crash of receiver into the cradle. Brad's feet hit the floor simultaneously.

The peal of bells sounded again.

"Hello," Brad ventured cautiously.

"Mr. Coleman. Is it true . . ."

Brad swore, slamming the phone down and pulling the plug from the wall jack. Padding to the bathroom, Brad doused his face with cold water then brushed his teeth and rinsed his mouth. He walked the long length of his cream-colored hallway to the compact kitchen. After turning on the percolator, he downed a tall glass of orange juice and had started on another while returning to the bedroom where he reconnected the phone. He dialed a number and waited.

"Good morning. Brooks & Brooks. May I help you?" the pleasant feminine voice answered.

"Good morning, Phyllis. Has William gotten there yet?" Brad asked gruffly.

"Oh, Mr. Coleman. No. He just called. He's on his way. He asked me to let you know he'll be on time for your appointment. Is there any message?"

"Yes. Beep him please. Ask him to call me right away. Thanks, Phyllis," Brad said hanging up.

Brad picked up the phone on the second ring, saying, "William?" The voice on the other end was smooth and unrushed. William Brooks, the son and junior partner of Brooks & Brooks answered, "Yes, Brad. What's up?"

"Those damn reporters," yelled Brad. "You assured me before I left for Virginia the story was squashed. The very day I got there, Helen called to say a reporter was nosing around her trying to sniff up something. Now this morning all hell broke loose. What happened?" Brad barked into the receiver.

"Brad. That's why we're meeting in my office today, remember?" The calming, almost drawl of the voice of Brad's friend and attorney had the desired effect its owner intended and Brad quieted. "I've just pulled into the garage, Brad. Hang up, stay away from the phone and TV, have yourself a cold shower and take your time getting here. We have all day," William ended, hanging up his cellular car phone.

William Brooks rode thoughtfully up to the twelfth floor suite of offices in the Adam Clayton Powell, Jr. State Office Building which housed the law firm of Brooks & Brooks. The firm had been founded by William's father when William was still in grade school and was now respected throughout the city by its corporate clientele.

"Hi again, Phyllis," he said to the mature, mahogany-skinned woman who greeted him with a pleasant smile. "Phone driving you nuts?" He gave her a wide grin and a conspiratorial wink. His secretary grinned back good-naturedly. "Stark-raving," she answered. Then, seriously, she stated, "It's pretty bad this time, Mr. Brooks."

William looked at the concern on her face. Nodding, he echoed, "Pretty bad this time," entered his office and softly closed the door.

Following his attorney's advice—partially—Brad took a cold shower, sat down with a second cup of coffee in the living room and disobediently turned on the TV. Switching channels with the remote, he stopped at a news station and waited. Finally, the TV journalist said, "Bradford Coleman of fast food fame is in the news again. Last week we reported that the same bizarre case of food poisoning that nearly killed a patron five years ago has been repeated, this time leaving two patrons near death. A spokesman for Mr. Coleman and the TAMA Corporation stated that Mr. Coleman is out of town and cannot be reached for comment."

The screen darkened as Brad pressed the remote's off button. He sat silently, his brooding dark eyes narrowing to slits, his brow wrinkling in thought. Finally, he stirred, walked to the kitchen phone, dialed a number and waited.

"Hello."

"It's Brad, Helen."

There was a small pause, then softly, "How are you, Brad?"

"Surviving," Brad spoke gruffly. "Helen, I'll be with William most of the day. Can we meet this evening?"

The strained voice prompted Helen's soft reply. "Of course. My place. Come when you can."

"And there you have it. The whole story up to now," finished the attorney as he closed the bright red folder on his desk. Both men sat facing one another in deeply tufted black leather chairs. In similar positions, elbows rested, laced fingers supporting chins, they stared at one another, Brad's angry eyes meeting the watchful gaze of his friend.

"Incredible," Brad finally spoke. "Ptomaine poisoning! And they're absolutely certain of the source? Dammit, William," blasted Brad as he stood up, thrust his hands in his trouser pockets and strode to the window.

Brad stared out at the throngs of people and traffic below on busy 125th Street, Harlem's cultural corridor. His eyes flickered over the Plaza, taking in the lunch-break office workers seated on the flat, red granite planters. Brad always found this street a fascination. Where else but in a stretch of seven blocks from Third Avenue to Adam Clayton Powell Jr. Boulevard, would you find interaction amongst such a diversity of cultures?

The office workers, without walking far, could purchase from street vendors a myriad of goods: an exquisitely carved ebony statue from West Africa; gaily patterned cloth from East Africa; malachite from Nigeria. Crossing the street to enter the Studio Museum of Harlem was yet another world of delights. To see an art book written and illustrated by Black writers brought forth a burst of pride. Brad admired the tenacity with which the small businessman survived, competing daily with the large franchisers along the strip.

His gaze lingered on a fast food franchise located a few doors away from the Museum. It had changed little since the summers he'd worked there while still a college student. Later, when he'd decided to remain in the business, he had been the store manager. His eyes softened as he remembered the pride he had felt and the determination that one day he would own a franchise. He'd worked long, hard hours to succeed, and succeed he had. At the expense of family . . . Laura . . . the image of his dead wife was replaced by his last look at Julia's anguished face as she ran from his embrace. Julia . . . he thought. What could she be thinking now about his mess? Will she listen to me? Allow me to explain? She will. She must.

Eyes darkening, he said to William, "You know what a tight ship I run, the people I employ. No. I refuse to believe my employees' negligence is the cause," he finished harshly, turning to face his attorney.

Leaning almost casually against the window frame, hands still thrust into his pockets, his eyes blazed as he spoke. His voice, now quiet, had an ominous quality. "I do not want this to go as far as a trial this time, William. I want whoever is trying their damndest to ruin me, stopped. *Now.*"

William Brooks sat watching his friend and client as he stared out the window. The relaxed pose was a facade, for William knew his friend well. He knew the pocketed hands were clenched fists. The throbbing temple and pulsating neck muscles indicated the tension he knew his friend was feeling.William had seen it before–five years ago when Brad's businesses nearly folded because of similar bad publicity. That time, he knew Brad had felt pain and disbelief at the betrayal of a supposed friend and colleague; this time, William sensed the quiet fury boiling in Brad's gut. He knew that this time, Brad would leave no stone unturned in finding those bent on destroying him.

Since the deaths of Brad's wife and chilren in the car accident, William had watched his college pal metamorphose from a happy businessman to a cold, calculating machine who ultimately became highly successful and respected in his business world and in his community.

William's deep brown eyes shone brightly in his dark burnt-umber face as he watched Brad return to his chair and fling a leg over its arm. In answer to Brad's remarks, his alert eyes fixed on Brad's angry ones, he said, "We've got people working around the clock. JJ's report will be here in the morning, " he continued, referring to the private investigator employed by his firm.

"JJ," Brad echoed, visibly relaxing at the mention of the name. JJ was the energetic, intelligent head of the firm named simply, 'Investigations/Jerard Johnson.' "JJ?" Brad's voice was filled with expectancy. He had been impressed with JJ's efficiently-run operation since they had first met several years before.

"Yes." William smiled and nodded when he saw his friend's taut shoulders loosen. "He's on to something," William continued.

"Who's responsible?" Brad asked, his voice low.

"Not yet, Brad," William said firmly. "Everything is inconclusive. We're proceeding carefully on this. When I read JJ's report, you'll be informed," William concluded.

"Does he name names?" Brad prodded, his stare penetrating.

"Yes," replied William simply.

Brad sighed, knowing that was all he was going to pry from his friend. The integrity of the firm of Brooks & Brooks was well-known. Brad knew the attorney would not jeopardize that reputation with premature details given to an angry client bent on swift action.

Brad shifted his position on the deep mammoth burgundy

couch, sitting up and swinging his stockinged feet to the floor. Helen placed the food-laden tray on the table in front of Brad, then sat down across from him on an identical couch.

Tucking her legs clad in filmy pants beneath her, she settled back, silently watching Brad eat. After a few moments, Brad looked up at Helen, gave her a broad wink and said, "You do it every time, dear friend," and continued chewing the savory meat from the succulent barbecued rib.

Helen Stevenson, the mother of Brad's dead wife Laura, smiled, her eyes growing warm as she watched the man who had been her son-in-law enjoy her cooking. She'd teased him once about being a closet eater. "Ribs and fried chicken at my place—hamburger specialties in public," she'd joked.

"Image. Must think image," Brad had teased back.

Now, as he downed the last of his cold ginger ale and wiped his mouth and fingers, she started to get up to remove the tray and refill his glass.

Brad stood, giving her a look that said sit still, and deftly picked up the tray, taking it to the kitchen. He returned with a Heineken for himself and a diet Pepsi for Helen. Brad took a long swallow before putting the glass on the table, then flopped full length on the couch, lacing his fingers behind his head. Some of the tension began to leave his body; he felt no need to engage in conversation until he was ready, and he was not pressured into doing so. Brad was at peace here. The room was made for comfort. With eyes clouded, he could recite every detail of the huge living room in the old whitestone house. The soft banana-colored walls were strewn with family photos as well as art by Bearden and Feelings. The burnished exposed ceiling beams give a vintage look; a scattered array of old and new objects were pulled together by multicolored oriental carpets over polished hardwood floors. Brad had fallen asleep on the huge wine-colored couch many times over the years when he had succumbed to mental and physical fatigue.

He opened his eyes now, looked at Helen and smiled. She was reading. He continued to look at that woman who had helped bring him back to sanity after he had lost his family. As if *she* hadn't needed consoling with the loss of her only child and grandchildren. He gazed at her silver hair: premature graying, a family trait. She wore it chemically straightened and very short, full on top and tapered at sides and back. Her warm, beige-brown face was free of wrinkles but sprinkled with tiny black moles. Her striking appearance would be considered handsome rather than pretty.

When she reached to take a sip of her drink, he grinned. Helen was of average height, but her erect carriage gave her a taller appearance. She had never been slender but carried her extra weight well because it was evenly distributed.

Helen glanced at Brad when she felt his eyes on her and noted his grin. She put the book down and grinned back, her diet beverages a joke between them.

"Okay, okay," Brad said. He laughed. Noting the quirk of her brow and her pursed lips, he began to fill her in on the details of his visit with William Brooks.

"Is that it? Is that all?" Helen said, her hand rhythmically slapping her trousered thigh in an impatient gesture. "Almost two weeks and all he has is a report from JJ?" She ended with a final slap on her leg.

Brad sat up. Planting his feet on the floor and resting his elbows on his knees, he said, "Take it easy Helen. Believe me, William's not dragging his feet on this. I trust him," he said quietly.

"Well," Helen continued, "the name? Any hint at all that Charlie Pierce is at it again? You know he hates you."

"No, Helen. It's not Charlie Pierce, as you and I first thought. William's no fool. Pierce was checked and ruled out immediately. As we know, his lifestyle for the past few years has been less than glamorous. No. He's not involved this time. When he was paroled, he headed for Arizona and is still there working as a limousine driver."

"But who . . .?" The agitation in Helen's voice was not unnoticed by Brad.

"I know–me too," he added in a low voice.

Helen studied Brad, noting the bitter edge of cynicism in his tone. She tilted her head to one side, staring at him, her eyes questioning. But Brad had dropped his head in his hands and did not see the sudden concern cross her face. Helen feared the miasma that had struck Brad twice before in the last six years was about to hit again. This time, she knew she would not be able to cope with it as well as she had done in the past. His pain would be too great and he would need more than her motherly hugs for consolation. Helen's glance flickered over the wall of photographs. Laura, her daughter, Tasha, Omar, her only grandchildren . . . dead. She stared at the picture of her beautiful daughter, the cause of all their deaths. Helen remembered that rainy March night when Brad called her from a Riverdale Hospital. She had learned when she arrived that Laura and four-year-old Omar had been killed instantly when the car skidded into a utility pole. Her six-year-old granddaughter had to be pried from the wreck. She had found Brad at Tasha's bedside where he had remained for nine days until she died, never regaining consciousness. Her beautiful, spoiled, selfish daughter, snuffing out three young lives because of her vanity and her immature inability to become a reasoning adult. She had suddenly become the party girl . . . parties without her husband.

Brad looked up. His eyes followed Helen's to the wall of pictures. A shadow fell over his face, his mouth becoming a grim line.

"We've talked about this," Helen spoke softly. "The hurt will never leave you."

Brad stood up and walked to a table, picked up a small silver frame, then returned to the couch, staring at the image of Tasha. "She would be twelve this year," he said, his voice growing husky. Then, his voice soft, he said, "I saw a little girl just that age a few days ago in Norfolk. Tasha would be doing those same things now–running, swimming, just beginning to find out she's a feminine little girl." Visibly shaken, Brad set the frame on the table and strode from the room.

Helen's eyes misted as she watched him go. Since the deaths, she and Brad had comforted one another over the years, becoming friends. She had watched the pleasant, optimistic, open young man who had married her daughter become a cynical, hard, mistrusting man. He had never allowed himself to become close to another woman, especially if she was as beautiful as his dead wife. Toward the end, Brad had suspected Laura's unfaithfulness, her falling prey to the attention from lustful admirers.

Helen went in search of Brad, finding him sitting thoughtfully on a lawn chair in the small, neatly-gardened back yard.

Brad gave Helen a smile that reached his eyes. "I'm fine," he said, in answer to her unspoken question.

"I know," Helen replied, satisfied that he was recovered. They sat in silence, listening to the summer evening sounds common in midweek in a working-class neighborhood. After a few moments of silence, she said, "Is she kind, compassionate, good to her parents?"

Brad instinctively found himself nodding to Helen's question before he realized its impact. His mouth opened and a laugh bellowed up from his gut, his eyes twinkling. His infectious laughter caught and Helen found herself shaking with glee. She wiped at her eyes and said, "This is old Helen here, remember?"

"Old what?" scoffed Brad. "At 57? Please! But how did you know that it was special this time?" Brad asked, wondering, thinking of the dates he'd brought to various functions at Helen's.

"I'm a woman," said Helen, hardly able to contain her mirth.

"Helen," growled Brad in a menacing tone.

"Well," Helen began, sitting down next to Brad on a matching lawn chair. "The first clue was, exhausted as you were when you arrived from Paris, you met with your attorneys and then *drove* to Norfolk, all in two days?"

"But—," Brad began.

"But, nothing," Helen resumed. "Now I know your little friend Samm´ was good company for you in Paris. She was homesick; you took her under your wing; befriended her. But all that for a picnic?"

"She's delightful, Helen," Brad said simply.

"Yes, and you speak of her as if she were a kid sister, too."

Brad smiled as Helen continued.

"The second clue was when I called you at Sammí's parents' home to tell you that all hell had broken loose in the media. After you quieted down, what did you say? 'Not now, no, not now.' At first I was puzzled," Helen went on. "But then, the third clue was when you said, 'I can't leave yet. Julia's coming,'" Helen ended, repeating Brad's words. Now, staring intently at Brad, she said, "Did I get the name right? Sammí's sister's name?" Her voice trailed away.

"Julia."

"Uh huh," Helen said triumphantly, when Brad repeated Julia's name. "Fourth and final clue." She slapped her knees, looked at the bewildered Brad and said, "Well. Is she?"

"What?"

"Kind, compassionate and good to her parents?"

"Yes," said Brad slowly, thinking back to the last few days spent with the Hart clan. Julia's warm greeting to her parents, the love she and Samantha shared, the twins' adoration of her. "Yes," he answered softly. "She's all that." He looked at Helen. "Why?" he asked.

Helen's eyes filled with warmth and moisture. "I prayed so hard for you all these years, Brad. When I saw you close your heart to the world, I began to pray. So now it's happened. You've fallen in love."

Brad nodded unconsciously, in agreement with Helen's statement, "It's amazing, Helen. This feeling . . . it's almost as if I knew this was going to happen. All the stories told to me in Paris by a lonely young woman . . . her family, her sister," Brad said, his voice strained. "I was fascinated," he continued. "I had to meet her. When I met her, my expectations were justified. In three days . . . three days," Brad repeated, "I had fallen in love. In *love*," he whispered, facing Helen in awe.

"She's beautiful," Helen's voice was factual.

"Gorgeous," replied Brad, raising a brow in question at his friend. "I . . ." he started, but never finished.

"You fought yourself," Helen supplied. "Beautiful women can't be trusted," she said. "That was your cloak of protection all these years." After a few moments Helen reached over to pat Brad's hand. "You're looking mighty fine in your new garments," she whispered, her eyes moist. Then, straightening, she asked, "Does she know?"

Brad gave Helen's hand a tug. He got up and began pacing around the fenced yard.

"What happened?"

"She thinks I'm in love with Samantha."

"That baby?" shouted Helen.

"Hardly a baby at twenty-four," said Brad dryly.

"Never-you-mind," Helen said. "Where you're concerned, she's a baby. Now, what happened? Why didn't Sammí tell Julia the truth?"

Brad sat down on the grass, arm resting on one raised knee, the smell of new grass and flowers reminding him of the knoll in Virginia. Slowly, he began to relate the events of last week, ending with the fateful embrace, Samantha's revelations, and finally, his leaving without saying goodbye to Julia. When he finished, neither spoke.

"God in Heaven!" Helen finally exploded.

"What?" the surprised Brad looked up.

"That poor girl," Helen said clucking her tongue. "You left, not saying a fare-thee-well? Don't you realize that when you and Sammí didn't show up right away that she probably was thinking the worse? That poor girl," Helen said, shaking her head.

A sudden swell of despair coursed through his body at Helen's words. When he and Samantha had returned that night, he'd hoped Julia was waiting up for them. But as they entered the silent, darkened house, his heart sank. Sam had whispered, "Don't worry, you'll see her in the morning." Brad had lain awake thinking of the turmoil he'd caused Julia earlier. He had decided he did not want to see hatred reflected in her eyes. When he arose the next morning, only Mr. Hart had been up to see him go. "She was terrified, Helen," Brad said. "I had caused her to dredge up that old memory. She looked at me as if she were seeing that jerk," he finished, making a fist and pounding it into the palm of his hand.

"Maybe she did wait up for awhile," Helen said thoughtfully. "She probably realized her actions had puzzled you . . . that Sammí would offer an explanation. But . . . you'll never know . . ."

Brad thought about the level-headed Samantha. He remembered her remarks about the family's acceptance of him. His eyes glittered. "Julia knows now," he said. His voice held an underlying excitement.

"Brad?"

Brad looked up at Helen.

"You don't want to lose her," she said simply.

Brad smiled, got to his feet and kissed her forehead. "I don't aim to be doing that, dear friend. I'm going home to make a long distance call." With a quick hug, Brad whispered, "Thank you," and was suddenly gone.

Chapter V

Julia returned from the restroom in time to see Samantha scribble her autograph for a woman who strode back to her table, her grin triumphant. Samantha looked up as Julia reached the table, an apologetic smile on her face.

Julia patted Samantha's hand, saying, "That's the price of fame, dear. Enjoy it now," she ended, giving her sister a tweak of the cheek.

Samantha's face broke into a broad grin and her eyes glittered. "A year from now she'll walk right past me without a glance, I'll be such a fixture in this place," said Samantha, nodding toward the autograph seeker.

Samantha's face was flushed with excitement.

"You don't sit still long enough to become a fixture," said Julia. "I don't know how you're going to make it through your lectures."

"I'll make it, Ju," Samantha said softly.

"I know you will, Sam, I know you will."

Julia's eyes left her sister's face and swept the restaurant. Yes. She could see Samantha becoming a fixture here. Although the restaurant was situated in close proximity to George Washington University where Samantha would be studying, it was not overflowing with students. It was small and quiet and though the tables were crowded, it was not stuffy. Intimate, it was still casual. It looked upon itself as the neighborhood eatery where one ate a meal unhurried, as Julia and Sam had done.

Their meal finished, Julia was on her second cup of coffee, while Samantha sipped cold club soda with lime.

Julia sighed as she looked around the room. The admiring glances in their direction did not go unnoticed by Julia. Samantha had been recognized by the patrons and many sent nods and smiles towards their table. Julia was glad that they were left alone so that they could enjoy a quiet evening together before driving back to Norfolk in the morning. Julia was tired, but her sister could hardly contain her excitement. Samantha's school entrance interview earlier had been a success even though only a formality. She had already been accepted for the next spring term, and needed only to clear up a few minor details.

When Samantha had finally told Julia about her plans, Julia was at first surprised, then miffed that she hadn't shared in the planning, then happy about Samantha's decision, knowing all too well about the short-lived careers of models.

"You know these bones and this face are quickly aging, Ju. Soon they'll be throwing me out to pasture . . . before I'm thirty, for sure," Samantha had joked.

Julia had exclaimed, "That won't be for years, Sam."

"Only six," Samantha replied softly.

Julia had felt proud of Sam's decision to leave her modeling career and study full-time in her chosen field of cultural anthropology. Sam had always been a bright and inquisitive student. Her determination to succeed had been proven by completing two years of undergraduate requirements by independent study and taking some required lab courses in Paris. Over the years Sam would mention she was taking a course here and there but never let on she was attaining her degree.

Yes, Julia was very proud of her baby sis who knew what she wanted and had set out to achieve her long-range goal. Sam had told Julia that her only regret was that Julia, who had been busy building her own career, had never visited her in Paris. Now that Sam would be leaving Paris in six months, they'd never stroll down the Avenue d' Champs Elysees on the way to the Arc de Triompe or see the art at the Louvre or in the subway at the Gare du Nord or visit the Eiffel Tower or enjoy a *croque-monsieur* on the Left Bank. Sam's suggestion that Julia end her four-week vacation in Paris was tempting, but Julia had demurred. Now, as they sat leisurely sipping their drinks, Sam prodded, "Why not, Julia Hart? You always promised you'd visit me in Paris. If you don't come now, we'll *never* be there at the same time. You'll be running your new department and I'll be deep in required reading," Samantha pleaded. Then with a mischievous grin and raised eyebrow, she said, "You hurrying back to New York–would it have anything to do with our conversation two days ago?"

Julia ducked her head and blushed as she busily folded and unfolded her napkin, avoiding her sister's query. A smile tugged at the corners of her mouth as she thought back to two mornings ago, the day she awoke to find Brad gone. She was sitting at the table having coffee with her father when Samantha came bouncing down the stairs, kissed her father and questioned him about the missing Brad, having knocked on his bedroom door and receiving no answer. She was told, as Julia had been a few moments before, that Brad had left very early, saying that he'd call. When they were left alone, Samantha, noticing Julia's reserved manner towards her, began her persistent questioning of Julia. The relentless questions caused Julia to blurt out, "I'm sorry, Sam. I never meant for it to happen. You know I would never hurt you. I'm happy for you," she finished, her voice breaking.

Samantha, realizing from Brad's remarks the night before the misconception that Julia had about them, had said, "Julia, you're wrong. I'm such a silly goose. I should have seen a little quicker than I did what was happening between the two of you." Sam's eyes had softened when she saw the look of disbelief on Julia's face. She said, "Ju, I'm the younger sister he never had."

Julia had said, "But last night when you came home so late, I thought . . ." Julia had ended, not able to say the words.

Then Samantha had related the details of the conversation. Samantha had told of the anguish Brad felt at dredging up the old Ralph Manning hurt. She'd told Julia of the look of fury in Brad's eyes when he heard of Manning's crude behavior toward her. She'd also told Julia of Brad's unspoken reply when she asked him if he loved Julia.

Julia's heart beat had quickened. Brad in love with me? Julia had thought.

Now, in answer to Samantha's question, Julia said, a smile in her voice, "Since you have to rush back to Paris, I've decided to finish my vacation in New York. You know how I love the concerts in the park, the street fairs . . ." Julia's voice trailed off.

"Yes," said Samantha. "You're going to love them even more with tall, dark and handsome at your side, too." She ducked as Julia made a mock swing at her chin.

"Come on, fresh pot," Julia said. "We'd better get back to the hotel and get some sleep. It's been a long day and we've got to get on the road before the rest of the world does."

As they walked to Julia's car, they passed an apartment building where the doorman was standing outside. He smiled at Samantha and she waved. "I'm going to love it here," she said.

Earlier that day they'd visited a rental agent who had shown Samantha several condos in the area, two of which were located in the building with the friendly doorman. Samantha had registered with the agent who promised to find the right apartment at the right price. She would not have to "worry about a thing" he assured her.

Back at the hotel, the desk clerk gave Samantha a message saying Brad had called. "Will call back," the note read. They rode up to their 12th floor suite in silence, both women lost in thought.

Well, of course he would ask for Samantha, Julia thought. The suite is registered under her name.

Samantha thought, What if he's angry that I told Julia how he feels about her?

As Samantha put the key in the lock, the phone rang.

"Hello," she said, breathlessly.

"Hello, Sammí," Brad said, using the French pronunciation. "Has everything gone well?" he continued, his voice controlled.

"Yes," Samantha said hesitantly. Brad seldom used her professional name. Puzzled, she asked, "Is anything wrong, Brad?" She could have kicked herself. After seeing the news broadcasts for the past two days, how could she have asked that? She said, "Oh, Brad, I didn't mean . . ."

"Forget it, Samantha," Brad said softly. "We're trying to iron this thing out as quickly and sanely as possible." He was silent until Samantha finally said, "Brad . . ."

Brad spoke, "Sam, . . . uh . . .is Julia . . . uh, is she . . .?"

With a grin and a sigh of relief, Samantha said, "Brad, she knows I'm just your kid sister and I sorta think she likes the idea. Hold on a sec, she's right here."

When Samantha picked up the phone, Julia had waited, but when she heard Samantha say Brad's name, she had left the room. She was sitting quietly on the bed when Samantha poked her head into the room. "Brad's on the phone. He wants to talk to you," Samantha said.

Julia looked at Sam, her eyes questioning.

"Go on, girl. The man's waiting. And close the door on the way out. I do think you'll want some privacy on *this* call," teased Samantha.

"Hello." Julia's voice was soft, wavering just a little. She wondered what to say to him.

"Julia."

At the sound of his voice, a warm glow sped through her body.

"Julia," he began again in a huskier tone. "I'm sorry I left without seeing you, but it was important that I return to New York immediately."

"I know, Brad. We've been watching the news here. I'm sorry," she finished softly.

"Julia. I . . . on the boat. I didn't know."

She was silent.

"I would never knowingly hurt you. You know that, don't you?" His voice was a gentle whisper.

"Yes."

"When are you coming home? I want to see you."

"My plane leaves Wednesday; I'll get into La Guardia around noon." Julia became silent. How could she tell Brad that she wanted him to meet her at the airport and drive her to her apartment where she could hold him tightly in her arms? When she thought of lying in his arms on the knoll in Virginia she ached with the need to be enfolded in those arms again.

"Julia," Brad's voice broke into her thoughts. Then, almost as if he'd read her mind, he said, "Is anyone meeting you? Can I pick you up at the airport . . . take you home?"

"No." When Brad said nothing, Julia hastily corrected herself.

"Uh, no . . . I mean, no one is meeting me. Yes. I would like you to pick me up, Brad. I would like that," Julia said, her voice a murmur.

"I'm glad. I'd like that very much. I . . . Julia . . ." Brad's voice trailed away.

"Yes, Brad?"

"Julia," Brad began, "did Sam . . . uh, have you and Sam talked?" His voice died again.

Julia smiled. "Yes, Brad. Sam and I have talked," she replied simply. She could hear Brad catch his breath. Then, his voice barely a whisper, he said, "Would you like me to make lunch reservations or would you prefer to go right home?"

"I'd like to be taken right home, Brad," Julia said.

After a moment, Brad said, his voice husky, "Home it is then. 'Til Wednesday."

After giving Brad her flight information, they both said goodbye.

Brad lay back on the bed, his long legs crossed at the ankles, his head cradled in his clasped hands. He was taunted by the image of Julia, the sound of her voice.

As Julia followed her fellow passengers down the long corridor to the baggage area, butterflies played tag in her stomach. She took small swallows to ease the dryness in her mouth. Drawing a deep breath as she passed through the doors leading into the waiting area, she glanced around, scanning the expectant faces of the crowd waiting for the arrival of friends and relatives. Craning her neck as she was pushed towards the baggage carousel, Julia frowned in disappointment at not being able to spot Brad. Perhaps he couldn't make it, she thought. Visions of him being detained by a last-minute call flashed across her mind, causing her brow to wrinkle. Sighing, she watched the carousel move slowly. Spying her one bag, she started to reach for it when a strong, muscled, mahogany arm appeared, lifting it easily off the conveyor belt.

"This it?" Brad said, his brow raised quizzically.

"That's it," she breathed softly, her eyes suddenly sparkling.

"That's better."

"What . . ."

"Your eyes. Keep that smile in them. For a minute there, when I spotted that frown, I had second thoughts about coming over. I thought maybe you had changed your mind about my meeting you." His dark eyes were smiling.

"No."

With her nylon bag in one hand and his arm touching her elbow, he guided her to the exit doors. Nodding at the bag, he said, "Do you always travel this light?"

"Most times. When I'm working, all I need is a change or two. Wash and wear. The rest is usually my equipment and I carry that on board."

Julia hoped the beat of her heart was not audible to Brad's ears. Her step was light as they walked towards the exit. When she thought she was not going to see him, a quick case of the blues had overcome her; then when she heard his voice and saw his handsome face, she wanted to throw herself into his arms, to kiss his strong mouth. The short-sleeved yellow shirt tucked into the light gray slacks fitted to his torso, showing the well-formed muscular arms and thighs. He struck such a handsome figure that passing females threw him seductive smiles and backward glances. She felt a twinge of jealously even though Brad, perfectly aware of his admirers, kept his eyes straight ahead, guiding their path through the crowd. Once he winked at her, giving her elbow a gentle squeeze.

Outside, Julia began to look for his bright red Cougar. She was puzzled as Brad started to guide her towards the row of waiting limousines. Stopping at a long, navy-blue stretch Lincoln Town Car with a black leather top, he greeted the driver who was holding the door open. The driver, tipping his black cap with the leather bill, was impeccably dressed in black tailored trousers and a pale blue short-sleeve cotton shirt.

"Thanks, Roy. What's this?" Brad said, taking the piece of paper from the driver's extended hand. As the driver helped Julia into the car, Brad read the note. "Damn," he muttered, jamming the scrap of paper into his pants pocket and sliding into the seat next to Julia.

Noticing the look of puzzlement on her face he finally said,

"I'm sorry Julia," knowing she was probably wondering about the limo service and his reaction to the message he'd just received. With a gesture indicating the limo he explained, "I thought we could have a relaxing ride uptown. Talk without interruption—no traffic bobbing and weaving–no noise. No searching for a parking space on 79th Street at high noon. I call Roy pretty often when I have to get around the city. I hope you don't mind," Brad said, hoping to dispel any fears she might have that he was putting on a display for her benefit.

Julia smiled at Brad, settling back as the car left the curbside. "No, Brad. I love it. What woman wouldn't like being whisked off in a fine chariot like this . . . with a charming knight to boot?"

Brad, relieved at Julia's upbeat response, reached for her hand, squeezing it, "But..." he began, a frown creasing his forehead.

"I know," Julia said, indicating the scrap of paper he had stuffed into his pants pocket. "A change of plans?" she asked.

Still squeezing her hand, he replied, "A perceptive lady. Yes," he answered. "Do you mind? It's just a slight detour, then we'll be on our way."

"No problem."

Brad called to the driver who had driven nearly out of the airport complex. On instruction from Brad, he closed the glass privacy panel. Brad sat silent as he watched the driver head for the parkway to Brooklyn. Then he saw Julia's look of concern; he reached over, and with one finger under her chin, turned her face towards him.

"We're going to my apartment. The message Roy received on the car phone is from my attorney. There's a courier camped on my doorstep, waiting for some documents. I was supposed to leave them with the doorman before I left. But in my haste to be where I am at the moment, I completely forgot." Brad leaned over and lightly brushed his lips over Julia's. "I'm sure," he continued, "if William were here now, I'd be promptly forgiven my absentmindedness."

When Brad's lips touched hers, Julia fought to control the surge of passion coursing through her. A moment before, when he had squeezed her hand, a warm shiver had traveled from her toes to her head.

Brad, not realizing the havoc he'd created with just a few gestures, sat back regarding her, his gaze filled with tenderness. "I'm glad you're here," he said softly.

Julia, struggling for a normal voice, said, "Brad, the case. I haven't seen anything more about it. Does that mean it's been resolved?"

Brad's face took on a grim look, his eyes darkening. "It means the vultures are lying in wait for more fodder to feed their voracious appetites. The patrons are no longer near death and appear to be recovering, so we've lost the center stage spotlight. For now."

Hearing the bleak sound, Julia's heart ached for him. His pain was her pain. But how could she tell him? Wordlessly, she reached over and touched his hand.

Brad's eyes filled with warmth at the tender but shy gesture. For the rest of the trip, they spoke of safe matters, Julia's family, the reunion, Samantha's surprise and sudden return to Paris.

They watched the driver wind his way through the busy Atlantic Avenue traffic, effectively dodging the bullying truckers and the rude, careless speed-plowers. Soon the car pulled up in front of Brad's apartment building on Cadman Plaza in Brooklyn Heights. It was a modern building and well-kept, its occupants running the gamut from middle-class working people, to the well-to-do, to retiree. Brad had bought the apartment in an attempt to remove himself far from the existence he had known as a husband and father in Riverdale. Though he was known throughout the complex, he was allowed his privacy, along with other celebrities in residence.

Brad left the limo and spoke to the doorman who introduced him to the courier waiting in the cool lobby, then returned to the car.

"Julia," he said, opening the door and helping her out. "I know you're famished by now. What do you say to having Chinese food in? Then when this heat breaks, I'll drive you uptown."

Julia was hesitant in replying.

Brad took her silence as a negative response. He said, a sigh escaping his lips, "Okay. Bad idea. Just wait for me here. I'll be right down with the documents for the courier."

As he started to turn away, Julia touched his arm lightly. She pointed to the trunk saying, "My luggage."

When Julia hadn't replied immediately, Brad's heart sank. He thought bitterly, "She doesn't trust me yet." But at her touch and her words, his heart skipped a beat.

After taking the luggage from Roy and watching him drive off, Brad, Julia and the courier rode up to Brad's twelfth floor apartment. He gave the documents to the man, watched him walk down the carpeted hallway back to the elevators, then softly closed the door. Standing just inside the apartment foyer while Brad gave instructions to the courier, Julia glanced around the spacious apartment. Her look was one of admiration and appreciation as she noted his choice of colors. The room was a composition in brown and white, offset by deep-pile abstract-carved soft mocha carpeting. Two long couches seemed to fill the enormous room. Covered in heavily textured Haitian cotton, they were separated by an equally long white-marble parson's table. Each couch was flanked by identical tables, a heavy, crystal-base lamp with chocolate-brown shades on each one. Brown, white, cream and beige pillows were strewn on both couches. On the white-textured walls were colorful contemporary paintings. Julia recognized some of the work: two Otto Neals were displayed prominently.

Walking into the room to view the other paintings, she read the name of Tom Feelings, then, kicking off the sandals, she turned her attention to the window. It was a glass wall with a glass door opening onto a terrace. Sheer white voile draperies billowed slightly from the air conditioner current. Gazing in awe at the panoramic view, she felt Brad standing beside her. She hadn't heard him walk up to her; he too had removed his shoes and the heavy carpet had muffled his footsteps.

She smiled at him, waving her hand towards the terrace saying, "Great view. The bridge must be wonderful to see at night." The Brooklyn Bridge was in direct view of Brad's window.

Brad drew the drapes apart for a clearer look. "Yeah," he said. "I enjoy it—especially at night. It's beautiful. If you really want to see it in all its glory, watch on a snowy night, late—hardly any traffic to disturb the new white blanket–the snowflakes drifting lazily past the lamps. What a sight! Something you must see."

Julia laughed at his enthusiasm. "O.K. I certainly will plan to make it here one snowy night."

His laughter filled the big room. "I got carried away, didn't I? All right. No matter what we're doing, that first snowy night belongs to us."

"Deal."

As their gazes met, they burst into another fit of laughter, both thinking of the mid-July heat and the sweltering streets below. Brad dramatically mopped imaginary sweat from his brow as they chuckled at their silly moment. He guided her to the couch where they sat down.

"What's your preference? Food," he said, answering her questioning look. "What do you like? Seafood? Chicken? Beef? They make great lobster dishes. My favorite is stir-fried lobster with black bean sauce. Their shrimp dishes are mouth-watering too."

"Stop. I can't stand it. How about Szechwan? I'd love some Szechwan shrimp."

"Great choice," Brad said, reaching for the phone on one of the smaller tables. He punched in a number and then listened. Soon he was giving his order. When he hung up the phone he turned to her. "Something cold?" he asked.

"Bordeaux?"

"Coming up." He walked the few steps to the kitchen separated from the living room by a long, beige, enameled breakfast bar with matching beige high-backed stools. The appliances were almond and white. The terra-cotta floor was in marked contrast to the pale furnishings.

After a moment he returned, carrying a bottle of Chateau Meyney and two crystal glasses, one a long stem for red wine. Walking to a long wall on one side of the room, he opened a burnished walnut cabinet, intricately carved, removing a bottle. He poured wine for her, then Hennessy for himself. He returned to sit beside Julia, handing her the chilled glass.

"Delicious," she said, after taking a sip of the fruity beverage.

Brad watched as she sipped the wine. She had unabashedly tucked her feet up under her and was settled back into one corner of the couch. Sitting so close to her, not touching for fear of earning her mistrust, caused him agony. He wanted to crush her to him, to taste her sweet mouth again. But he would not. To cause her uneasiness on unfamiliar territory was unfair. Instead, he said, his voice husky, "I'm happy to see you again. I've missed you."

Julia looked at Brad. Before he had spoken, she wondered why, now that they were alone, he hadn't attempted to kiss her. Since their meeting at the airport, their looks, their touches in the car, however innocent, the magnetism between them was unmistakable.

Now in his apartment, he appeared to have put a veil between them. He was so close yet so far. For the past two days following Sam's revelations, Julia had thought of this meeting. Her feelings for Brad were so strong that she knew if there would be but one kiss, one caress, her good sense would become captive to his touch.

But, she puzzled, his sudden reserve was mystifying. Frowning, she thought, Did I misinterpret Sam's words? Was Brad pitying me? Her mind was racing. I know he cares. I heard it in his voice, saw the look in his eyes. I know he missed me. She closed her eyes in agony. "Oh, Brad, I've missed you so much." Julia gasped when she realized she'd spoken aloud.

"Julia?" Brad was surprised to hear the anguish in her voice. The small sob that escaped her lips wrenched his heart. "Julia," he said again, reaching out, his large hand tenderly turning her face to him. Her eyelashes were moist. "What did you say?" Brad asked, not understanding, but wanting to ease the pain.

Her look was intent as she straightened her shoulders. "I've missed you," she repeated in a strong voice that conveyed the unmistakable message she was sending.

Their gazes locked, each searched the eyes of the other for a long moment. There were no misread messages.

"Sweet Julia," Brad murmured, as he pulled her into his arms. He kissed her damp eyelids, the tip of her nose, her cheeks. He brushed her lips gently, then hungrily his mouth captured hers. "If only you knew how much I've wanted you, needed you. It's been too long since I've held you . . ."

Julia felt herself drowning in Brad's embrace. Her body burned from the fiery fingers that were dancing on her skin. The penetrating heat smoldering in her caused her to gasp. She strained against him.

The sound of the buzzer jarred them to reality. Muttering, Brad strode to the intercom where he instructed the doorman to send up the delivery man.

Julia walked down the hall to find the bathroom. The room was startling, all gleaming chrome and gray marble. There she surveyed herself in the mirrored door. Her hair was mussed and she grimaced at her appearance. The tailored cream slacks and sheer off-white blouse had more than their share of wrinkles. Shrugging, she turned on the tap and doused her face and neck with cold water; her skin still sang from Brad's touch, her lips stung from his intense kisses. Opening the door, she saw Brad leaning against the wall, arms folded, ankles crossed. Neither spoke. Her mind remembered his touch and sent a message to her body, causing a movement of delicious warmth.

Finally he spoke. "The food's here. Ready to eat?" he asked bleakly.

Julia went to him. "No." She reached up and put her arms around his neck, pulling his head down to hers. "Shrimp Szechuwan is not what I want right this minute, Brad." Her kiss was soft and moist. "I want you. Don't you want me?" she whispered.

"Oh God! Want you?" Brad caught her to him, holding her tightly. "Want you?" he repeated huskily, as he inhaled the flowery scent of her. Moving swiftly, he picked her up, carrying her the few steps to the bedroom.

Walking across the enormous room to a huge over-size bed, he put her down, her feet soundless on the deep pile midnight blue rug. The colors of the living room flowed into the bedroom but touches of old blues in Aztec design dominated the covered headboard, the linens and the low, wide armchair.

Her arms still around his neck, she found his lips again. He caught her to him, his answering kiss filled with longing, his tongue reaching deep into the recesses of her mouth. He heard her moan as his hand moved over her breasts, the nipples already taut and straining through the sheer material of her blouse. Brad unbuttoned it, then pushing it from her shoulders and reaching behind her in one quick movement, he unhooked her bra, releasing her from the sheer lacy fabric. The cinnamon circle throbbed under his touch as he took a tender nipple into his mouth, running his tongue around it in a circular motion. "You're beautiful," he groaned as he tasted her. Gently he eased her onto the wide bed, lying beside her. Turning to him, she unbuttoned his shirt, her hands seeking his nipples, teasing each one until they hardened under her touch. Bending her head she slowly ran her tongue across one, then the other, allowing her teeth to close for the barest fraction of a second on them.

"What are you doing to me . . .? Julia . . . I can't stand this any longer . . ." His voice was gruff.

Julia responded by swirling her tongue on his chest and up to the soft hollows of his neck, her hands gently massaging his back.

Gasping, Brad said, "Are you sure? I didn't bring you here to . . . Julia . . . look at me."

Julia opened her eyes and looked at Brad. She said softly, "I know, Brad. I'm sure."

Brad leaned down and kissed her lips lightly. She began to remove her slacks. Catching her hands and pulling her to her feet, he said, his voice a ragged whisper, "Let me do that."

Julia stood while Brad undressed her. His hands slid down her naked breast to her slim waist where he unfastened her slacks, letting them drop to the floor. His fingers looped over the elastic of her panties, sliding the wispy bit of cream silk down over her hips. Sliding with them as they dropped, he lifted her feet out of them, one at a time. Slowly rising, raining little kisses on her calves, her knees, her inner thighs, the scent of jasmine and her moist flesh driving him wild, he whispered her name. Pausing just above her curly mound where he felt her throbbing pulses, he slid his tongue up and across her smooth belly. Reaching her breasts, once again he suckled them.

Julia thought she could stand it no more. She wanted to feel him inside her.

"Brad," she moaned.

"I know, my sweet, I know." His mouth pressed against her throat, he unbuckled his belt, letting his pants fall to the floor and swiftly removed his briefs. When her curly hairs brushed his nakedness, his groin quivered and he grew hard against her. With a rumble starting in his throat and escaping as a primal groan, he eased her back on the bed, positioning himself over her. Tiny sounds burst from her lips as his hands moved magically over her body sending millions of hot tender sparks through her. His mouth moved over her skin as if trying to taste every inch of her. When she thought she would explode with longing, he lowered himself. Her gasp was filled with expectant pleasure when she felt his hardness.

She grasped his chest, arching her body to meet his. He guided her hand to him, encouraging her to touch, to explore. When her fingertips brushed him he groaned, crushing her closer, so they seemed as one.

Brad could feel the passion of Julia's arousal so much that every shiver of her body sent an electric jolt through him, causing him to call out with his need.

"Julia?" he questioned.

"Yes—yes—" Julia cried.

"Soon my love." Deftly he reached out, opening the bedside table drawer and removing a foil packet. Protection in place, he eased himself once again onto Julia's hot flesh.

"Brad," she pleaded, opening her legs for him.

Responding, he entered her. She gave a little cry as he pushed through the tight canal. Thrusting deeply into her, he could feel the searing flames of her need.

Brad's throbbing passion ached to be released. His thrusts sent tidal waves of sensual pleasure to Julia as she rhythmically met each one.

Their bodies were an exquisite meld. He could feel her inner heat enfold him as he drove deeper into her, gathering all her sweetness. He wanted to wait for her though his pain was sweetly excruciating. He whispered, "Sweet, I can't hold back . . . are you . . .?"

"Now, please now . . ."

She arched to reach his deepest penetration, her legs wrapped tightly around him. Finally, with a great shudder, moving in unison, their passion exploded in fragments of delightful, intoxicating quivers–a kaleidoscope gone crazy.

Quietly, moments later, Brad eased himself off Julia, but never let go, holding her close. Her eyes were closed. Lightly kissing her eyelids, her forehead, he murmured, "My sweet lady," then lay back, his chest heaving rapidly.

Julia sighed, snuggling closer to Brad, her head resting on his rising chest, the curly hairs tickling her nose.

Brad smiled at the soft sound. He squeezed his eyes shut, hugging her tightly. My God, he thought, I love this woman. She's what I need, what I want. She will not get away from me. But how to let her know without scaring her off? His thoughts raced. Only days ago she thought I was her sister's lover . . . and now this scandal. Brad's smile became a frown as he thought of the media, how they never failed in their hyped reports to play up his bachelor lifestyle, digging up stale clips of beauties clinging to his arm. No, he thought, his eyes darkening, I will not ask her to share my life with these debacles intruding at every turn.

His eyes filled with warmth as he made his decision. He lifted Julia's face to his. The smile in her eyes and on her lips stabbed his heart. No, my love, he told her silently, I don't mean to lose you when I've only just found you.

Chapter VI

Julia awakened, remembering instantly where she was, the realization sending a surge of warmth through her body. Realizing Brad was no longer lying beside her in his king-size bed, she turned her head to look for him. He was standing with his back to her, looking out of the wide picture window. The bright sun was forcing its way through the chocolate-colored vertical blinds. He'd changed into lightweight beige cotton slacks and a pale blue, short-sleeve jersey. Apparently he had showered, for the faint scent of soap and lime drifted towards her. He stood casually, hands in pockets, deep in thought. At his feet was her travel bag which he'd brought in from the living room. Watching him undetected, Julia allowed her eyes to roam freely over his well-toned form. Only a short time ago, those muscled legs and arms were entwined with hers while his hands did wondrous things to her body, evoking pleasurable sounds from her, one of which she made now at the vivid memory. Embarrassed as the sigh escaping her lips caused Brad to turn from the window, she groaned again, trying to slide underneath the sheet as he started towards her.

He looked down at her, arms folded across his chest. "That bad, huh?" he asked, his voice stern.

"No," Julia blurted. "It was . . . I mean . . ." She stopped when she saw the laughter in his eyes and his mouth begin to broaden in a wide grin.

Flustered, she flung a pillow at him. It bounced off his broad chest as he bent over, kissing her lips lightly.

"I know. Me too," he murmured against her mouth. Tenderly he cupped her chin in his big hand forcing her to look at him. Their eyes met and locked.

Julia read the message and her heart sang.

"Sweet Julia, my sweet Julia." He kissed her long and hungrily. Releasing her gently, he stood up, his fingers lingering lightly on her cheek. Huskily, he said, "If I don't let you nourish that beautiful body of yours I'm going to be arrested for physical abuse, my sweet."

At that moment, Julia's stomach growled loudly.

They both burst into laughter.

Brad, still laughing, handed her a robe. "You'll find everything for your shower in here," he said, guiding her to the bathroom. "By the time you've finished, the food will be warmed." Pulling her to him by the lapels of the robe, he said, "No need to take the time to change. You need food . . . fast." He kissed her forehead as his fingers lightly feathered her breast, then released her saying, "Be gone with you."

Adjusting the shower nozzle to its fullest spray, Julia tilted her head, allowing the cool waterfall to pelt her face. She turned and twisted, the spray cascading down her neck and back soothing her heated skin. Reluctantly, knowing that Brad was waiting, she turned off the water and stepped from the shower stall, reaching for the fluffy burgundy terry towel.

As she toweled her hair and patted her skin dry, she caught her own gaze in the mirrored door. Her face was flushed and her dark eyes glistened. She grimaced at the message she was reading in them. Holding up a finger and pointing to her reflection she said, "You're heading for a nasty fall, Julia girl. Shake the stardust loose. Careful now . . ." She frowned, turning her back on her full reflection and looked into the mirror over the basin as she finger-fluffed her dark curls. No, she thought, he never said that he loved me. He never mouthed the words but his eyes spoke volumes.

She could still feel the taste of his sweet mouth. Her cheeks burned hotly when she thought of their lovemaking. She remembered how she had snuggled into his arms as if that had always been her rightful place. Just as she had drifted off, she felt his lips caress her forehead and could hear his low whisper, but she'd fallen off to sleep without hearing his words. Perhaps he did say he loves me, Julia thought wistfully. She shuddered as she pulled on the robe, tying the sash around her slim waist.

As she walked down the hall to the kitchen, the pungent aroma of the Szechuwan shrimp assailed her nostrils. Just as she reached the kitchen where Brad was taking plates from an overhead cabinet, her stomach grumbled again loudly.

He turned around at the sound, grinned, throwing his head back with a great burst of laughter. "All right, miss, I hear you," his voice tenderly teased. He patted the seat of a high-backed stool. "Here you go. Sit right here."

As Julia seated herself, the oversized robe fell open, revealing a generous portion of her breast.

Brad's appreciative look was not missed by Julia as she pulled the robe together. His grin was broader as he winked an eye, spreading his hands in a helpless gesture.

"Well, it was your idea for me not to take time to change," she smiled sweetly.

"I get such great ideas at times." Reaching out, he lightly caressed her cheek. "Let's feed that stomach of yours."

After they had cleared the dishes, Julia returned to the bedroom where she dressed, then taking her luggage, she walked down the hall to the living room where she found Brad sitting on the terrace in a lounge chair. He stood up, giving her an admiring look.

Julia had changed into a cool-looking, sleeveless mint-green dress, drawn gently at the waist, accentuating her hips. The neckline was gracefully scooped. Her long legs were bare and she wore the same tan flat-heeled sandals she'd kicked off earlier. Reaching for the tall glass of cold iced tea Brad handed her, she sat down, looking around at the panorama before her. The haze over the bridge, the cars looking like so many tiny scurrying bugs, the mingled sound of the street traffic below and the airplanes above creating their own curious music.

"I love your view," she said. "You're right in the midst of loads of activity, yet up here you're apart. So peaceful."

"I often sit here whenever I'm home. The scene never bores me with its constant changes." He looked at the bridge then at Julia. "The first snowfall. Remember!"

"The first snowfall." Her voice was a whisper. Then, placing her glass on the table, Julia stood up. "My plane landed at noon and it's nearly five. I'm sure by this time, Mr. and Mrs. Hart have listed me as a missing person. I always give them a call when I return from a trip."

Brad reached for her hand, stopping her from leaving the terrace. "Must we end it now?" His voice was low, his eyes questioning. "We've all night, tomorrow, the rest of the week. You're still vacationing, aren't you? Unless you've made other plans . . . with someone else . . ." he ended abruptly, dropping her hand.

Other plans? Someone else? Julia's thoughts echoed Brad's words. Aloud she said, "No, Brad. No plans. No someone else."

With an audible sigh, Brad led her from the terrace into the cool living room. "Then your time is my time for the rest of the week, lady. We'll start right now."

"But. . ."

"I know," he said, steering her to the phone beside the couch. "Call your parents. Be sure to tell them if they can't reach you for the next few days that you're in safe hands."

Brad wielded his bright red car onto the West Side Highway, becoming part of the uptown rush hour traffic. The air conditioner was off and the windows were rolled down, allowing the warm evening breeze to brush them fleetingly.

Julia watched Brad deftly avoid roadhogs and annoying tailgaters, his arm muscles flexing lightly with each movement. She wanted to reach out and touch him but did not, settling for just looking and remembering. After she had made her call to her parents, Brad had taken her bag and they left the apartment. He said nothing as they took the elevator down to the basement garage, walked to his Cougar and within moments were driving effortlessly on the busy streets, winding their way to the Brooklyn Bridge.

Now he smoothly changed lanes and exited at 125th Street.

"Harlem?"

"Uh huh," Brad said. Noting her quizzical look, he said, "No, not work, Julia," realizing she knew his lawyer's office was on 125th Street.

"It's Wednesday night," he continued.

"Grant's Tomb. The Jazzmobile."

"Smart lady," Brad grinned at her.

Julia grinned back, settling against the soft leather seat, her eyes full of delight. "I'd forgotten. This *is* the first night. Who's playing?"

"Can't say. No schedule. But more than likely it'll be a crowd-pleaser. Mungo, maybe. Or Jimmy Heath."

Brad glanced at her. "Do you come every Wednesday?"

"No, not every week. Most times I'm tied up at work and can't leave in time to catch a set. Last year, I made it twice. How about you? Were you here last year?"

"I never made it at all. I was in Paris a good part of the year."

Julia fell silent as Brad began looking for a parking space two blocks from the Tomb, on Broadway and 121st Street. Though the concert started at seven o'clock, at six-thirty, finding a spot to park was next to impossible. To Julia, summer wasn't complete unless she spent time at the Tomb, listening to the jazz greats. Since her first summer in New York, she'd been attending. She loved the camaraderie of the crowd. Strangers speaking to strangers, the chance to hear the young, future greats, the food vendors' cooking sending tantalizing aromas wafting through the air. The sidewalks became a marketplace for exotic baubles and paintings by up and coming talented Black artists. The vast display of books by Black authors, the skillfully-crafted greeting cards and beautiful jewelry never failed to heighten her sense of cultural pride.

And now to know that Brad shared her enthusiasm for this Harlem event brought a soft smile to her lips.

Brad noticed the smile as he helped her from the car. Locking the door and pocketing the key, he said, as he took her arm, "Want to share?"

"I just had this thought that over the years we've probably passed one another several times–or shared a step," she said, referring to the stone steps leading up to the monument.

"Or I was the guy who couldn't take his eyes off you," Brad teased. He squeezed her hand and she answered with a firm tug. His chest heaved and his groin ached as he longed to pull her close and kiss her tender lips. Instead, he cleared a path for them up the steps and almost to the top of the Tomb, squeezing into a space barely large enough for them both.

"You're right," Julia said, pointing down at the Jazzmobile which was already in place at the edge of the expansive stone-paved clearing. She read the names of the performing artists. "Percy and Jimmy Heath."

"Partly right." Brad grinned, apparently pleased with his guess.

Neither of them hungry, they had agreed to forego the food vendors until after the concert, but they were finding it extremely hard to do, being surrounded by the delicious smells of food. Brad groaned as the man next to him removed the foil wrapping from his plate, allowing the pungent aroma of barbecued ribs to drift skyward.

"Man, you're just too cruel."

"Didn't have a choice, brother. No willpower," the man said, a friendly grin splitting his face.

"Know what you mean," muttered Brad. He turned to Julia, giving her a wink, and slipped her hand into his as they gave their attention to the Heath brothers' opening rendition of an old Charlie Parker tune, "A Night in Tunisia."

The phone started to ring just as Brad put the key into the door lock. He picked it up on the third ring. "What's up, William," he asked, recognizing his attorney's voice. Brad was silent for long moments as he listened. Finally he spoke, "No, William. I told you a few day's ago–the name David Jensen still means nothing to me. Since you asked, I had a profile check run in all of my businesses. I got zip." He paused. "JJ's absolutely certain? Yes . . . I know how thorough he is." Brad listened again, a frown puckering his brow. Closing his eyes, he rubbed his hand across his lids. My employees are above reproach, he thought. What is William trying to prove? Me interrogating them about a stranger—still—. "All right, William, if you think it will do some good. Friday?

Absolutely not! William, listen to me. I'm not leaving before Sunday and that's final." Brad listened awhile longer before he said, "Sunday, William. I'll ring you before I leave." He hung up the phone.

"Damn," he muttered, striding to the living room where he flung open the doors of the walnut cabinet, his well-stocked bar. After fixing a gin and tonic, he carried it to the terrace where he sat thoughtfully staring at the kaleidoscope of lights flashing by on the bridge. "Damn," he said again, as he mulled over William's words. How could he just pick up and leave for Paris? To leave Julia... The sound of his balled fist hitting the palm of his hand shattered the quiet of the terrace. He took a long swallow of his drink, setting the glass heavily on the frosted glass table. Whoever said, "Life's not fair," would be rich as Croesus if he owned the patent on the phrase, Brad swore. After awhile his anger subsided when he thought about the unfairness to two innocent people who had nearly bought death when they patronized his store. His anger surfaced when he thought about the greed of his competitors. To flirt with the possible deaths of innocents for personal gain and power—Brad's disgust with his fellow humans burned his gut. Resigned, he knew he must go to Paris to substantiate JJ's suspicions. According to the detective, he'd turned up an interesting bit of information in Paris concerning one David Jensen, an employee of Brad's main competitor who'd opened a store there within a few months of Brad's Paris franchise debut. JJ had brought back a picture which William was sending over in the morning.

"Maybe this guy was a former employee under a different name," William had said. "There's got to be a connection."

Brad frowned. He did not want to leave Julia. How could he tell her he was flying out of her life after all the plans they'd made tonight? His eyes glowed as he thought about their evening together. After the concert, famished, they'd made a hurried scramble through the thinning crowd to purchase fish dinners. After eating, they browsed through the remaining vendors. He had bought a pair of handcrafted silver earrings that she admired for Julia and J. California Cooper's latest book for himself.

After seeing Julia to the door, sorely tempted to invite himself in, he had kissed her, then left, content that they'd be breakfasting together in the morning. "And now this," he said aloud in disgust.

Julia stretched languidly on her queen-size bed, wrapping her arms around fluffy pillows encased in white cotton percale, lavishly embroidered and edged with scalloped lace. Her one indulgence was luxurious bed linens, and she owned a wardrobe full, changing them to suit her whims. A large antique steamer trunk against one wall of her generous-sized bedroom was filled with sets of linens in all colors and prints. No matter what color she chose, it complemented the room, which was all ivory: lace curtains, carpeting, walls. Shelves were built into her walk-in closet just for her matching comforters and bedspreads. During the summer months she used all white sets, some covered with Laura Ashley's pale prints and Sheridan's bold ones.

Now, she pulled the matching lace-edged sheet up to her chin and dreamily closed her eyes, a tiny smile playing about her mouth, images of Brad filling her brain. What a glorious vacation I'm having, she thought. Yesterday, wonderful yesterday. She blushed, remembering the visit to Brad's apartment. Brunch today, sailing tomorrow. What Saturday and Sunday would bring—who knows? She smiled, snuggling deeper into her pillows.

During the drive home last night she and Brad had planned the rest of the week. She marveled at the ease with which they began mapping out their time together—as if it was the most natural thing for them to do. As if they'd been doing it for months, not just two weeks . . .

Just as she flung back the sheet and her feet hit the deep pile carpet, the phone rang.

"Good morning, Brad," Julia said, a frown puckering her brow. He should be on the way here, not on the phone. "Is anything wrong?"

Hearing the concern in her voice, Brad said, "Everything's fine Julia. It's just that I'm afraid we'll have to turn breakfast into brunch. My attorney is sending over a package. It's important that I be here when it arrives. I'm . . ."

"Yes, Brad?"

"It's nothing," Brad said, his voice tensing. I refuse to spoil our time together, he thought. I won't mention Paris to her—not yet.

Finally, he said, "Is brunch OK? I want to see you," he ended, his voice low.

"That'll be fine. Brunch is even better. I found quite a few messages on my machine when I got in. Now I'll have time to answer them." She laughed. "Who knows? They may have replaced me. It feels like I've been gone forever."

"They wouldn't dare."

"Oh, you don't know the publishing world. A bud today, a faded rose in the morning," she quipped.

"Never you, my sweet, never you," he whispered softly.

The husky timbre of his voice over the wire and so close in her ear, sent a tickle of excitement through her.

"Eleven, then?"

"I'll be waiting."

Julia sat on the bed staring at the phone for a few minutes before she padded to the bathroom. He seemed, she searched for the word, preoccupied, she decided. She shrugged. After all, he did have a lot on his mind . . . and he's waiting for a package. His lawyer must think it pretty important to have called him so late last night.

After showering and dressing, Julia went to the living room to make her calls. She'd selected blue and white-striped cotton shorts with a short-sleeve matching jacket and a while sleeveless tee. Cutout flat white sandals completed her outfit.

Reaching for the phone and dialing a number, her brow puckered into a frown. I wonder what Jim Anderson wanted. As far as he knows I'm still in Virginia, she thought.

"Jim Anderson," Jim's voice was deep and melodious. He knew how to use it effectively in his relationships.

"Jim. It's Julia. What's the idea of bothering me on vacation? How did you know I was home anyway?"

"Julia. I miss you already, hon. Come back, come back," he pleaded in falsetto.

Julia laughed at Jim's foolishness. He tended to be the office cheerer-upper, the one who successfully smoothed ruffled feathers.

She said, "I'm supposed to be away, remember?"

"I called your folks, Julia."

The smile left Julia's face. Jim would only do that in a dire emergency, like the time she'd had a change of flight at the eleventh hour and was stranded in San Francisco during the holidays. The telephone lines were in such a mess she had asked Jim to try to reach her parents and inform them of her arrival a day late.

"Jim, what's happened?" Her voice was anxious.

"You may have to cut your vacation short, hon. You'll be moving into your new office sooner than you expected."

"Jim . . ." Julia's voice was threatening.

"Joe's had a stroke."

"My God," Julia exclaimed. "When? Is he all right? Jim . .."

"Easy, easy, Julia. He's OK. He's home now."

"When did it happen?"

"Soon after you left. The day after, actually. It was mild–there's no paralysis. He's moving slow, but he's going to be fine."

Julia relaxed. Joe Belknap, her friend and mentor. Since her first week at *Rags*, after he had seen her work and potential, he had started grooming her to make her mark in the company. Julia had grown fond of him over the years. She respected his work and his judgement. She had come to terms with herself about the giant step up in responsibility as the senior associate—the spot that Joe would vacate when he retired in September. When she returned from her vacation in early August she would move into his office where he would ease her into the routine of the demanding position. But with him ill . . .

"Julia?" Jim's voice broke in on her thoughts. "I know your mind is working overtime. Calm down. The department is in good hands–mine," he said.

"Finally," Julia said trying to keep her voice light. She knew Jim had wanted the position badly but had conceded when she was chosen.

"Only until you return, Julia. Joe made that clear. His doctor ordered light duty when he returns in a month. That'll coincide with your return, so you have nothing to worry about," Jim ended, his voice becoming kind.

"Thanks, Jim."

"Look, hon, I've got to run. The kiddies need me. We'll talk soon, OK? Enjoy the rest of your time off. No telling when you'll be able to leave this madhouse again." He hung up before she could reply.

She sat still, holding the phone in her lap, thinking. Jim was a real friend. Joe was right to leave things in his hands. He was good. But she was Joe's choice to take over. After the decision had been made, she and Jim remained friends as well as colleagues. She recalled the hectic early days. She and Jim had hired on as photographers within weeks of one another and had become fast friends as well as co-workers on special assignments. Quite a few times Jim had crashed on her sofa when they had to make an early flight or had to catch a sunrise shoot in mid-town. He lived in Yonkers, and many times he made an appointment by the skin of his teeth. Though he'd tried the romance route with her, they didn't click. Now, they were two friends who happened to work together.

Julia roused herself and made two phone calls. The first was to the florist. She ordered flowers to be delivered to Joe. The second was to Joe. His wife would have allowed Joe to talk, but Julia stopped her, saying to give Joe her regards and she'd talk to him soon.

Still feeling a little dazed at the news, Julia began aimlessly to straighten up a room that needed no straightening. She punched pillows on her sofa, fingered her plants. She peered closely at her plants for fungus, knowing she'd find them completely healthy, thanks to the twins.

The twins were retired schoolteachers, Letitia and Matilda Baldwin, who lived across the hall from Julia. The sixty-six-year-old sisters had never married. Friendly to everyone in the building, they had become fond of Julia when she came down with the flu. Living alone, helpless, she'd dragged herself to their door nearly in tears because she was too weak and unable to nourish her body properly. All she had wanted was a bowl of hot soup. She nearly fainted at their feet before she got the words out. With the soup came lots of friendly affection. Whenever Julia left town, she gave them her keys to empty her mail box and water the plants. She in turn looked after their aged cats whenever needed.

The sound of the buzzer made Julia jump. It was the doorman announcing Brad's arrival.

When Julia reached the lobby she could see Brad through the glass doors, leaning casually against his car, arms folded across his chest, legs crossed at the ankles. Dark glasses shielded his eyes from the strong morning sun. He smiled at her, nodding his head, watching her approach. When she was close enough, he reached for her, taking her shoulders in his hands and pulling her toward him, planting a light kiss on her forehead.

"You look good enough to eat, and I'm starving," he murmured.

"I'm just as hungry as you are, so you better watch out," quipped Julia.

"Uh oh. What have we here? Have I created a monster? The lady on her own turf is ba-a-ad," he teased.

"That's right. Nothing like home ground to boost one's confidence," she teased back. If she could see his eyes behind those dark glasses she knew they'd be twinkling.

After helping her into the car then easing himself behind the wheel and fastening his seatbelt, he turned on the engine and pulled away from the curb.

"Confidence?" A smile played about his mouth. "Has one lost one's confidence? With *moi*?" Brad said, pointing to his chest. He removed his glasses and turned to glance briefly at her, his eyes serious. "Don't ever kid yourself, sweet Julia. You have all the confidence you'll ever need." He reached out and took her hand, brought it to his lips and kissed her fingertips, then placed it back in her lap.

"Want to talk about it now?" Brad asked softly.

Julia look up, surprised at his question. How perceptive he is, she thought. Are we that attuned to one another? The thought led her to counter, "I could ask you the same."

"*Touché*," he said, bowing his head deeply to her.

Her insight into his own change of mood moved him so deeply that a feeling of warmth flowed through his body with the speed of light, the tenderness he felt for her shining in his eyes. He wanted to crush her to him–feel that satiny skin next to his. Instead he said, a smile tugging at his lips, "No fair. I asked first."

She eyed him from beneath her long dark lashes. With a mock

sigh, she said, "Oh, then all's fair in love and . . ." her voice trailed away purposely.

"Julia . . ." His tone was threatening.

She laughed, her eyes bright, and, she hoped, not too obviously shining with love for him. With that thought, she turned her head, inspecting her surroundings. They were at Sylvia's on Lenox and 126th Street. They had arrived at the same time as the other early lunchers or late breakfasters–the two separated by their choice of orders. Brad had managed to commandeer a private corner table for them. He had given the waitress the order of chicken and waffles for himself, and pancakes, sausage and eggs for Julia. The diners surrounding them were a mixed crowd of families, singles, and mostly couples like herself and Brad. One couple seemed to be having their first breakfast together. They barely looked at their food and held hands across the table. She smiled at them, causing Brad to turn his head to look.

He turned back to her. "They're in love," he whispered, his dark eyes glinting as he stared at her.

"I know," Julia answered, suddenly embarrassed at the message she was receiving.

Brad reached for her hand. He massaged it gently, then spoke. "I'm waiting."

"My colleague, Jim Anderson, had bad news for me," Julia began. She related the content of her conversation with Jim, her voice breaking miserably when she spoke of Joe's illness.

When she finished, Brad, who never released her hand, squeezed it, his thumb moving back and forth over the tiny opal on her small left finger. "I'm sorry." His voice was full of concern. "Don't worry. I've seen people spring back from that sort of thing and continue normal activities. The man doesn't have to stop living–just slow down."

"I realize that," she spoke sharply. Immediately regretting her abruptness, she said, "I'm sorry. It's just that . . ."

He reached over and cupped her chin so that she was forced to look at him. "I understand what you're feeling. But you can do it. No need for guilt. Instead of Joe spending a month with you holding your hand, you may have to jump in feet first. You can handle it."

"You know that, do you?" Her audible sigh was full of misery.

"Sure." His eyes were twinkling. "Look at it this way. If you weren't the *man* for the job, there would be no discussion. Plain and simple." He shrugged his shoulders nonchalantly.

At his deliberate emphasis on gender, Julia unconsciously sat up taller in her seat, her eyes glinting dangerously, her lips tightening. Realizing that was his intention when she heard the laughter began to rumble in his throat, she laughed with him.

"That's my lady."

The tenderness of his voice covered her like a silken web–one that she never wanted to disentangle.

The waitress brought their food and they ate in companionable silence.

Their meal ended with both sipping second cups of coffee. Julia said, "Your turn."

During their meal, Brad had carefully weighed the decision about not informing Julia of his trip to Paris. Convinced he was right, especially after her own disconcerting news, he was determined not to fill their last three days together with morose feelings. He would tell her on Saturday night when there would be only a few hours left before his early Sunday morning flight.

"Is it the case? Have matters gotten worse?"

Her soft voice broke in on his thoughts.

"I'm not sure," he answered truthfully. "The package I received this morning did contain some information my attorney wants me to explore thoroughly. He thinks I may have the answer without knowing it. I've got some homework to do, but I promised myself not to get started until Sunday." Which is true, Brad breathed to himself. "But, enough of business–for both of us. We're going to give this town a whirl. Right?"

His contagious enthusiasm was caught by Julia although she wasn't fooled into believing his whole story. True, he had heard from his lawyer, but she didn't buy his lighthearted scoffing about putting off his "homework". And suddenly she didn't care. When the time came he would reveal his concerns to her. Right now she was willing to fall under his spell and let fate take them where it would.

Dawn had barely broken when the buzzer sounded, disturbing the early morning quiet. Julia instructed the doorman to tell the driver she'd be right down. She grabbed her purse and dufflebag, gave the room the once-over for any forgotten item, then softly closed the door, locking it. She glanced at her neighbors' apartment door, grinning, never sure if the sisters heard her goings and comings or whether they watched her through their door viewer. They always seemed to know how long she'd been away and if she was alone. Lifting her travel bag, she thought, won't *this* knock their socks off! But she didn't mind; she was comfortable knowing that the two women were concerned about her.

When she reached the lobby she found Brad's driver, the same one who'd met her at the airport, waiting for her. His starched pale blue shirt, black tie and slacks were impeccably neat. He tipped his black cap, saying, "Ms. Hart," as he reached for her bag. His demeanor gave no indication of familiarity.

After helping her into the back seat and stowing her bag in the trunk, he slid behind the wheel and smoothly left the curbside. At 7:30 a.m., the early-morning rush hour traffic was heavy, but the big limousine had no trouble maneuvering to the FDR Drive downtown and across the bridge to Brad's apartment in Brooklyn. Julia smiled just thinking about him and their time spent together.

Julia was deliriously happy. The thought had hit her like the pelting spray of the morning shower. While toweling herself dry, she had told herself that she didn't know she had been *unhappy*, before she met Brad. Her life before him was fulfilling–but filled with her career. She had no love interest, had not even the slightest thought of finding one, and now she knew why. She was in love with Brad Coleman. She could admit that to herself now, secure in the knowledge that Brad was not Sam's lover.

She had suspected her feelings over a year ago when she had first looked at a photograph and become captivated by a pair of dark unsmiling eyes. The first time those same sad eyes lit up and laughed, her heart had quickened, aware that she alone had been the cause. Now, these past few days, those eyes were filled with warmth and laughter–and love–for her. But why, she wondered, wouldn't he tell her? A frown appeared on her face and she sighed, "I've yet to tell him, so I guess we're even."

Wistfully she put the puzzle from her mind and turned her thoughts to what lay ahead. What did Brad have planned for them today–and tonight–she wondered, thinking about her bag in the trunk. His last words when they parted the night before were, "Don't forget to pack a bag . . . swimsuit and stuff. My driver will pick you up at first light."

Each outing had been a delight. The Jazzmobile concert, breakfast at Sylvia's, a tour of the Museum Mile, then down to the seaport for an evening dinner cruise. And now . . . who knew what?

The driver pulled up to the entrance of Brad's apartment complex. He opened the door for Julia, helped her out, then retrieved her bag from the trunk.

Julia looked up to see Brad walking toward her, eyes intent upon her face. The tenderness of his gaze suddenly filled her with a sense of waiting.

When he reached her, he said, "Good morning," brushing her lips lightly with his. Then to the driver, he said, as he took Julia's bag, "Thanks, Roy. I won't be needing the car for the rest of the day. I'll be in touch." Brad cupped Julia's elbow and guided her towards the building. Noting her glance at the driver's dismissal, he said with a grin, "Don't panic, funny face. I'm going to feed you." Suddenly he moaned, lifting his face to the sky. "I never saw such a woman. All she wants from me is food. What have I done? What have I done? Gods, have you stripped me of my charms?"

Julia laughed, giving him a playful punch in the stomach.

"Brad Coleman, you're a nut." Putting her arm around his waist while they walked, she squeezed him tightly.

While they waited for the elevator in the spacious mirrored lobby, she said, "After all, you did promise me an exotic breakfast. I haven't had my coffee yet, after you swore it would ruin my palate for this mysterious meal," she complained. "But I'm warning you. I want more than a croissant and coffee . . ."

"Soon, my sweet," Brad said as they entered the elevator. "Soon you will have the magnificent," kissing his fingers in a French gesture.

Walking down the carpeted hall to his apartment, the most tantalizing aromas taunted her stomach.

"Coffee," she murmured.

When Brad unlocked the door, the delicate smell of almonds tickled her nose. She looked at him in amazement.

"You didn't," she exclaimed.

Brad made a sweeping bow as she entered the foyer."Welcome to *Chez* Bradford, *Mademoiselle*."

Chapter VII

"Hi, Helen," Brad held the phone on his shoulder while he prepared his coffee. "Wanted to catch you before you started out. Any fairs today?" he ended.

"Hi, stranger," Helen replied, sounding pleased to hear his voice. "Yes, there are," she continued in answer to his question. "But I'm working at home this weekend. Getting ready for the Atlantic Antic in September. That's usually a biggie. I have lots of repeat customers. Where have you been keeping yourself?" she queried.

"Busy." Brad chuckled. He knew Helen was dying of curiosity. Usually, he would stop by her place, stuff himself with her fabulous meals or call just to touch bases. He hadn't done either since he'd seen her almost a week ago.

Then, sheepishly, he said, "Uh, Helen . . ."

Helen waited, knowing that Brad was about to ask a favor of her. He was always the one to do for her, seeing that her needs were met. When it came for her to do for him, he wouldn't allow it. The few times he had asked a favor of her, he found it hard to utter the words. She thought of it as silly male pride taking over. Now, she said, "Yes, Brad. Can I help with anything?"

Brad smiled. Astute woman. "Remember the opal? Have you

set it?" he breathed, waiting for her answer. Hoping.

"The opal?"

"Yes. The black opal. The one you gave to me."

"Oh, yes. That was so long ago I'd forgotten. Yes, I believe I still have it here. I've never shown it. It *is* yours." Helen paused. "Would you be needing it now?" Her voice held a smile.

"Yes," he replied slowly. Then, more firmly, "Yes. I need it now." He heard the smile in her voice and mused over it. Three years ago, Helen had given Brad a beautiful black opal stone as a Christmas gift, to be placed in a setting of his own choosing. Brad had fingered the smooth iridescent stone. Brilliant light emanated from the gem, flashing glorious colors in blues, reds and golden yellows. He had marvelled at the fascinating stone, telling Helen that such a thing of beauty should be set in a dainty bed of gold, fashioned for the most delicate of fingers, not vying for attention over his big knuckles.

"Glorify its beauty in one of your designs," he had told her. He'd never though of it again, until now. He had found the delicate finger.

Helen broke into his thoughts. "When will you be needing it?"

"I'll be there later today. Is that OK?"

"Yes. Brad?"

"Yes?"

"She's going to love it. It's special."

Brad hung up. The lady's special too, he thought, images of Julia flashing before him. He recalled the smile that brightened her face, her large dark eyes mirroring the world; the habit she had of wiggling her pinky finger when she was eating; her *ravenous* appetite. He grinned. He loved teasing her about her love for food and the fact that she wasn't weight conscious like the rest of the world. She had told him then about her three-times-a-week exercise routine which enabled her to indulge in her "sweet binges", as she called them.

Brad was on his second cup of coffee when he called William's home, Saturday, one of William's rare days off.

"Hi, buddy," William said hearing Brad's voice. "All set for tomorrow?" Unable to detect Brad's mood from his tone, William wondered if he was calling to announce he had cancelled his trip.

The exuberant voice he heard next surprised him.

"Just checking on any updates since we last spoke, William. My flight leaves at 9:20 a.m. in case there are any last minute instructions."

"I have your schedule, Brad. I checked with your secretary. No, nothing's changed. I'll keep you informed."

"William, about the other night. I was a little abrupt. Sorry. It's just that I had made plans for the week. Things are working out now."

William Brooks sat staring at the phone for a few moments, his black eyes thoughtful. "I wonder who she is?" he mused, happy for his friend.

The coffee aroma drifting down the hall and into the bathroom caused Julia to hurriedly towel her hair. She inhaled deeply as she moved quickly to the kitchen where she poured herself a cup of the dark brew. The taste of the dark chocolate raspberry liquid brought a sigh to her lips. She carried the cup to her overstuffed sofa, kicked off her slippers and, tucking her feet up under her, settled back to enjoy the heady stuff.

The coffee evoked pleasant memories of the delicious breakfast she had enjoyed in Brad's apartment the day before. He had led her to the terrace, seated her, then prepared to serve. She exclaimed over the exquisitely thin ham *crepés* with succulent sausages and fluffy eggs. The table was covered with a pristine white-on-white cloth, while in the center, violets floated in a fluted glass bowl. Julia admired the fine porcelain china with the bold navy stripes and the delicate crystal stemware. "It's lovely," she had told him.

After a leisurely breakfast, Brad had driven them upstate, remaining mysterious about their destination, but had asked her if she remembered to bring her camera as he had suggested.

When they arrived on the grounds of the Moultrie Sculpture Gardens in Yonkers, Julia's eyes shone like a kid's on Christmas morning as she surveyed the spectacle before her. There were sculptures of every imaginable shape and size, including that of a great marble bear standing over a pond where geese and cranes swam about. The sculptures wound out of sight down paths of the beautifully landscaped grounds. The many groves delighted her eye with rare trees and plants. There were also water lily plants and birch trees. Julia immediately began shooting pictures of the gardens with their beautiful blooms.

The gardens were virtually deserted. The fact did not go unnoticed by Brad, who used the opportunity to plant little kisses on her cheek, neck and lips, while she was shooting. After they had lunched on cold chicken salad sandwiches and lemonade purchased on the way, they left the gardens. When Brad had said goodnight at her door, Julia was pleasantly exhausted.

They had agreed to spend early Saturday doing catch-up chores before meeting for dinner in the evening. Julia decided to do her laundry when Brad told her he would be at this office most of the day, since for most of the week he had been grossly negligent in clearing his desk. He promised he would leave in time to pick her up at six.

The phone rang, breaking into Julia's thoughts. After reassuring her mother that she was having a great vacation in "that overpopulated sweat box," she hung up, promising that she would call home soon. Julia smiled. Soon, to her mother, meant tomorrow. But Mrs. Hart was used to hearing from Julia at least twice weekly–until the past week.

Julia roused, dressed in cutoffs and tee shirt and prepared to take her laundry to the basement laundry room. When the laundry was done, Julia planned to make a quick stop at the supermarket and visit Joe before returning in time to dress for dinner. While she waited for the elevator, her cart filled with laundry, she wondered what culinary delight Brad had planned for their dinner. She groaned, thinking about her lack of willpower when it came to delectable desserts. Shrugging her shoulders, a mischievous smile played about her mouth. Stepping into the elevator, she thought, Oh, well, another day for the exercise routine.

Back at her apartment, Julia made a call. Joe's wife Jeannette answered and assured her that a visit at noon would be fine for Joe.

She began preparing her wardrobe for what she believed was going to be a very special evening. All week she had a feeling that Brad was trying to tell her something. She sensed that it involved his business, when he mentioned beginning his homework on

Sunday. A frown flitted across her brow. For the past week Brad's name was missing from the media headlines. She recalled seeing an article buried on the last pages of one tabloid reporting that both of the stricken customers had been released from the hospital.

The newspaper article had not surprised her; when she'd asked, Brad told her that he had visited them at their homes the week before she had returned from Virginia. She remembered that Brad had been reluctant to talk about himself and those visits, firmly discouraging further talk about the matter, reverting briefly to his somber mood.

Feeling his pain, she had boldly pulled his head to hers, kissing him long and hard. She had grinned at him when she saw the dark cloud leave his face, to be replaced by the light in his eyes and his infectious smile.

"Mission accomplished," she had murmured.

"Hello, Jeannette," Julia said, entering the cool foyer of the Belknap apartment.

"Your vacation is agreeing with you, Julia. Whatever you're doing, bottle it. You'll need it when you return," Joe's wife said, as she and Julia hugged.

"I can't." Julia laughed. "This is just one moment in time, as the song goes," she said, wistfully thinking of Brad.

"Sounds bad and that ain't good," sang Jeannette in a clear musical voice, her blue eyes twinkling. They both laughed as they reached Joe, who rose to greet Julia.

"So what do we have here? A couple of songbirds now?" he grumbled, hugging Julia and kissing her cheek. "Hey, kiddo, you're looking great. What'd you do, go and fall in love on me? Look at her, Jen. I ain't seen that look on a young woman's face since you fell for me," he said, as he settled himself on the sofa again, his wife sitting beside him. Julia sat across from them both in a high-backed wing chair.

"And it's a good thing too," Jeannette playfully tugged her husband's ear. "But you're right, Fred." She looked at Julia. "I thought the same thing."

Julia looked at the couple. "Fred" was the pet name Jeannette had given to her husband. She said he reminded her of the "Fred" from the old "I Love Lucy" show with his bald head surrounded by a fringe of hair and his paunchy stomach.

Jeannette, like Joe, had warmed to Julia over the years. The older couple had insisted upon including Julia in many of their non-business dinner parties. Julia enjoyed the couple and their friends, but she suspected that on a few of those occasions, Jeannette had been sneakily trying to match-make.

Joe was saying, "You've gone and taken your own advice, huh, kiddo?" His belly shook with laughter and his dark blue eyes crinkled until they nearly closed. "Guess we got to get you a new sign now."

"Now stop teasing her, Joe," a smiling Jeannette said.

Julia smiled too, thinking about the sign on her office desk. She had been a good listener, never turning anyone away when she sensed their need to talk. Once she'd turned a deaf ear to a friend and it had cost her a relationship.

She thought about the sign her secretary had printed and placed on her desk. It read, '*Julia Hart-Advice to the Lovelorn—Free.*' Tickled at the sign, she never removed it. If you could see me now, she thought. Who's going to advise me? Falling for a stranger in a photograph. And when the real thing shows up . . .

"So when are we going to have the honor?" Joe's voice boomed, startling Julia.

"What . . .?"

"He means, when are we going to meet him, dear?" Jeannette said, her big grin showing even white teeth.

"Oh, you two. I'm just having a marvelous vacation. I hadn't realized how long overdue I was," Julia answered, keeping her voice light. Her heart suddenly felt heavy with the thought that her summer romance could end this evening. Shaking off her doom and gloom mood, she changed the subject, inquiring about Joe's health.

Half an hour later, Julia was on her way home. Feeling a little melancholy after visiting Joe, she decided to walk up Broadway after leaving the Belknap apartment on 61st Street. When she tired of window shopping, she would catch a bus to her apartment on 79th and Amsterdam.

Impulsively, she stopped, looked around for a public phone and finding one, dialed her office number.

"Jim Anderson."

"Bingo! I sorta had an idea you'd be there." Julia knew Jim was as conscientious as she was and would do whatever was necessary to take up the slack in her absence–and now Joe's.

"Not burning the oil are you?"

"Hi, hon," Jim said.

She thought she could detect a smile.

"I was about to run out for a bite. What's up?" he queried.

"That's why I'm calling. I'm in the neighborhood. Want to meet me?" Then, "I just saw Joe, Jim."

Jim Anderson caught the note of concern in her voice. He guessed what she was feeling. "Yeah, I know, hon. Where are you?"

"Broadway and 62nd."

"Ummm. Look. Why don't you make it to Antonietta's. I should get there in about fifteen minutes. Order for me. You know what I want. See you in a shake."

Discarding the idea of taxiing to 57th and Seventh from his 47th Street office, Jim hopped on the Broadway bus, making it to the restaurant in record time. He saw her sitting against a wall at a table for two in the cool, softly-lit room. The pastel interior with its intimate contemporary decor and superb Italian cuisine made the dining experience an exercise in relaxation.

When she saw him she smiled. He looked great. His deep beige skin was sun-bronzed. His dark brown eyes crinkled when he saw her.

Jim Anderson walked the length of the room to greet her. If only . . . he mused to himself. But, alas, t'was not to be. He kissed her forehead and sat across from her. "You're looking great, kiddo," he said, allowing his eyes to rove over her in appreciation.

Jim did not miss the envious looks other men in the room sent their way. She's not mine either, gents, he muttered to himself.

Julia reached across the table and tugged Jim's hand. "You look tired. You're using the assistants, aren't you?"

"Yes. I am. But you know how that goes. I still like to stay on top of things, especially with you and Joe both gone."

At the mention of Joe's name, a cloud drifted over Julia's face.

"He was hit harder than you led me to believe." Her tone was accusatory.

"Didn't want to worry you," he replied as the waiter arrived with their order.

Julia had ordered grilled scampi and egg noodles for Jim, and a small mushroom and tomato appetizer for herself, explaining that she had eaten at Joe's. They both ordered red wine.

"Will he really be able to return in a month? He seems so drawn. The weight he's lost–he tries to pretend this is light stuff. But it's not, Jim."

"You're right, hon. I've been speaking to Jeannette. It was pretty heavy going for awhile, she said. She's up on it though. Privately, it will be more like two months instead of the one he thinks it will be before he returns to 'light duty.'" He continued, "So be prepared to jump right in when you get back."

"That's what I was afraid of," she whispered.

"What's this? Am I hearing defeat? Doubt? From the fearless up an' at 'em, attack'em Julia Hart?" He mopped his brow in a nervous manner, feigning fright.

Within minutes he had her laughing at his antics.

They rose to leave after their meal was finished. Jim had reassured Julia that the office operation was running smoothly.

It was only three o'clock and Julia didn't have to rush for dinner with Brad, so she decided to take a cab uptown. She and Jim had walked over to Broadway in the hope of finding one more quickly. Julia waited while Jim watched for a free cab.

She turned her head to find Brad, hands in pocket, standing beside her, watching her intently. Her heart thudded at the sight of him. Startled, but happy to see him she began to smile, "Brad, what a surprise, I didn't expect . . ." She stopped, the smile disappearing as he looked at her, dark eyes smoldering with anger, lips a grim line. His eyes flickered past her to Jim who had turned around when he heard Julia speak.

Brad turned his gaze back to Julia. "I'm sure you didn't," he said, his voice low. Then, his eyes boring into her, he said, "Cocktails before dinner?" His eyes never left Julia's. His jaw was rigid and his temples throbbed.

He's furious, Julia thought. But why? Then she understood.

What a dolt I am, he thinks Jim and I . . . She said, "Brad, I want you to meet my colleague, Jim Anderson. Jim, this is Bradford Coleman." Julia's tone was cool. How *dare* he think I'd have another date just hours before *our* date, she thought.

Brad removed his hand from his pocket and extended it to Jim. "Anderson," he said his voice mild, his eyes still hard.

Jim took Brad's hand, "Coleman." His eyes were full of curiosity.

With a flick of his eyes, Brad dismissed Jim and turned back to Julia. "Business at my offices," he said nodding in the general direction of some office buildings.

Julia nodded unsmiling, remembering that TAMA Corporation held offices in the vicinity.

Brad moved closer to Julia. His intense look roamed swiftly over her face, searching her eyes. Though he was now smiling, his eyes were cold.

"Are we still on for six?" His voice was low. Julia barely nodded, unable to speak.

"Good," he whispered. He cupped her chin, bent down and crushed her lips in a bruising kiss, reaching out to steady Julia as she fell back. "See you then," he said, as he strode towards the waiting limousine and stepped inside without a backward glance.

Julia watched him leave, her anger barely containable as Jim patted her shoulder, saying, "Calm down, kiddo. The tornado has subsided." He let out a long whistle. "Whew. So that's *the* Bradford Coleman?"

"Yes," Julia said, still staring in the direction Brad's car had taken. "Yes." Her eyes darkened when she thought about Brad's uncalled-for behavior.

"So that's the reason for my girl's golden glow," Jim said. "Whew," he repeated. "When you play, you play in the big league, huh?"

"Jim," Julia threatened.

He grinned. "I'm sorry, hon. You know I'm only teasing you. But, speaking of playing, that guy's definitely not play."

"What are you talking about?" Julia was not amused.

"Where you're concerned," Jim replied, "Coleman is playing hardball. Thank God it was just old Jim he caught you with. He could sorta live with that–just barely."

"Caught me with . . . he had no right . . . we've only been out a few times."

"Look at me, Julia." He smiled. "This is old Jim here, hon. The look in your eyes when you saw him was the look I used to hope for," he ended. "Now," he continued, "you go along home and get ready for that date. He'll have cooled off by then and be feeling pretty ashamed of himself. Bet on it. That brother's not likely to mess up now."

Jim whistled for a passing cab, put her in it and stood silently watching as the taxi drove off.

As her taxi made its way through the late afternoon traffic on Broadway, Julia's mind was a flurry of activity. Her thoughts alternated between fury and reason. Images of Brad and his glamorous women danced before her . . . his arrogance toward her . . . is that how he treated them? It was as if he expected me to fawn all over him at his bruising kiss, she fumed. Did he expect that of his women? How could he treat me that way? A frown flitted across her face when she recalled the anger she'd seen in Brad's eyes. She couldn't understand the unleashed fury. We've not made any claims on each other, she reasoned.

She kept mulling over his actions, trying to clear the mystery of his instant jealous rage. In their time spent together, she hadn't noticed a hint of a jealous streak. Even so, why the sudden exhibition? During their most intimate moments, he never indicated that he wanted her to see only him. Though Julia knew he was happy that there was no one else, he had never staked his claim where she was concerned. So why the he-man act now? She fumed as she left the cab.

Walking towards her building, Julia decided to call Brad and cancel their date. His inexcusable behavior still rankled. If the ghosts in his past haunted him so, causing his irrational behavior, she wanted no part of him or them in her life.

After holding the door for her, the doorman reached for a large bouquet of yellow roses on the desk just beyond the lobby entrance. Tipping his cap and grinning widely, he handed the flowers to Julia. The bundle was so large, she had to wrap both arms around them.

She didn't have to read the card that was stapled to the cellophane wrapping to know that they were from Brad. She managed to read the message as she rode up on the elevator. It read, "I've hurt you. Can you ever forgive me? Please say you will." It was signed simply, "Brad."

Unlocking her door through misted eyes, she shook her head in annoyance at her weak moment. When the flowers were thrust into her arms she thought, just like a man. Give a bauble or a sweet–and they're in. But she knew–her heart knew–that his words were real. "Oh, Brad," she sighed.

As she walked into the living room to get a vase, she saw the blinking red light on her answering machine.

She pressed the button. "Ju, where are you, girl? Why haven't you sent a hi?" Samantha's voice was simultaneously cheerful and pouty. "I've been working my butt off since I returned. My schedule gives me almost five days off next week. Ju, won't you please come? Please? I want to show you off to everybody." Then she giggled. "Or are you otherwise occupied?" Samantha had hung up in the middle of a deep laugh.

Julia grinned. Hearing her sister's voice unexpectedly brought back memories of their week together. She missed her. She did regret not having visited Sam in Paris. They would have had such great fun together. Her assignment had taken her many places, but France had not been among them. One day, she mused.

She listened, because there was another message about to play.

"Julia." Brad's voice was hoarse.

She flinched at the pain she heard.

"I'm sorry. Will you forgive me? I'm not going to try to explain away my rudeness to you. You deserve an explanation, but now is not the time." His voice dropped so low, Julia had to strain to hear. "I am asking your forgiveness." He hesitated. "I'm coming to you. If you won't permit me to enter–I'll understand . . ."

Julia stood by the phone for long moments after the last click of the machine indicated it had reset itself. Finally, she turned away, not picking up the phone to call Brad.

"Damn," Brad swore as he expertly maneuvered the car to the curbside and out of the fast-moving traffic. Exiting from the

Brooklyn Bridge he had felt the tire go flat just after turning onto Chambers Street. He inched along until he found a space to pull into. Finding one a block off Chambers, he parked the car. He muttered, hating the idea of riding on a donut at twenty miles an hour. It was already 5:30 and he knew he would be late getting to Julia's. He'd call her as soon as the tire was changed.

Moving quickly, Brad changed the flat tire. Throwing it in the trunk, he slid behind the wheel and pulled away from the curb. Slowly he drove to Reade Street, proceeding along the busy thoroughfare, keeping an eye out for a service station. He scanned the sidewalks for the familiar *"FLATS FIXED"'* signs that were abundant in every neighborhood. "But not when you need 'em," he fumed. Two blocks later he spied the white and black lopsided sign hanging off a post, with an arrow pointing to an equally dilapidated store front, proclaiming, "*We fix flats.*" "Thank you, thank you, thank you," he murmured.

While Brad was waiting for the tire to be repaired, he reached into the car for the phone and dialed Julia's number. He frowned when there was no answer. The message machine was off. He allowed the phone to ring several times before hanging up. He glared at his watch: at five past six, Julia should be there. Unless..."Payback, Julia?" he thought wryly.

On his way once more, Brad drove carefully but hurriedly, filled with the need to see Julia, to hold her close to him. He wanted to chase the hurt from her eyes, hurt he had put there. The sight of her with another man holding her arm, guiding her protectively, the admiring glances of male passersby–he had allowed his old feelings of anger and betrayal to surface, causing him to hurt Julia.

He shook his head in disbelief. The emotional high he had been on for the past week was incredible. She had been a part of his life for only weeks and yet, the thought of her gone, not seeing her again . . . he grimaced at the thought. He prayed that she did not look upon the flowers as some cheap trick. The phone message? Would she listen? Would she see him when he was announced?

His hands gripped the steering wheel. She *has* to hear me out, she will *not* get away from me, he agonized. Cursing for the lack of parking spaces, he circled the block several times before finding one almost a block away from the building. Brad parked the car, hurriedly walked to the apartment complex, and entered the lobby. Speaking to the doorman, he found himself holding his breath as the doorman said into the intercom, "Mr. Coleman is here."

Julia jumped when the buzzer sounded. Brad. It was 6:30 she noted, looking at her watch. I hope he's all right, thought Julia as she went to answer the buzzer.

When she had listened to Brad's plea for forgiveness, Julia's heart had softened. While showering, dressing, she had pondered over the possible reasons that would make Brad lash out so viciously. She prayed that his explanation would clear the feeling she had that she would never see him after tonight.

When she decided not to cancel their date, she became filled with anguish, realizing she had quickly made him a part of her life. The idea of losing him was unbearable, but Julia also realized that whatever was bothering Brad, whatever had caused him such pain in the past still troubled him deeply. He would *have* to let her help. "It's up to you, Brad," she had whispered. "It's up to you to let me in."

When Julia unlocked her door, she was immediately swept into Brad's arms. She flung her arms around his neck, holding him tight, tears feathering her long lashes. "Brad." Her voice caught in a sob.

Brad groaned as he squeezed her tightly, his head pressed close to hers. "Sweet Julia," he murmured. "Sweet Julia. You've forgiven me." His voice broke. "I thought I'd lost you." His mouth covered hers gently at first, then hungrily searching until he found her tongue.

Julia's responding kiss matched his in desire. He rained little kisses on her neck, her eyes, her ears. He found her lips again, kissing them tenderly. Her skin burned from his touch as though fiery tongues were dancing on her body. She moaned, holding him close, molding her body into his contour. "Brad," she cried, filled with her need for him.

Brad picked her up, kicked the door closed and carried her to the oversize sofa, where he sat down, holding her on his lap, his lips capturing hers in a searing kiss. His hand massaged her breast through the soft thin fabric of her silk dress, bringing the nipple to a taut bud. Impatient at not being able to feel her satiny skin, he reached behind her neck and pulled the zipper down, easing the soft fabric from her shoulders, revealing the white lacy bra. With one swift movement, Brad unhooked the back clasp. Julia shifted and the wisp of lace fell away, baring her breasts to Brad's lips. Like a suckling baby he tasted each one until they became turgid peaks. Nuzzling the hollow of her throat, intoxicated with her perfumed scent, he said, "I want you, Julia."

"I want you too," she whispered softly. Julia breathed deeply, thinking, Yes, I do want you, Bradford Coleman. I do need you, want you in my life.

Slowly, gently, Brad eased Julia off his lap and onto the sofa. Puzzled, she looked at him.

He saw her look and swiftly kissed her lips, tweaking her nose as he grinned at her. "You know I want you, my sweet. Oh, how I want you." Folding her into his arms, he said, "But not now. Not here. Not in a schoolboy rush. When I take you it will be slow and I'll do my damndest to make the sweet pain last a lifetime, my lady," he continued, his voice nearly a croon. "I have such plans for tonight. It will be special because I won't be seeing you for awhile–" He felt Julia stiffen as she looked up at him.

"Don't worry. It's that bothersome homework, remember? But I won't be far away from you. I will see to that," he said firmly, as he brought her hand to his lips and kissed her fingers. He smiled to himself as he thought about the precious stone in his pants pocket. "No," he repeated, "I won't be far away at all."

Julia sat up, straightening her dress. She stared intently into his eyes, her dark eyes glowing warmly. "You will never be very far away from me. Ever." Her voice was as soft as a caress.

Their gazes locked for a long moment.

Julia smiled suddenly, ruefully looking down at her wrinkled dress. "Look at me. I wanted to be beautiful tonight. I must change."

"You are always beautiful to me," Brad said, standing up and kissing her lips lightly.

"Umm," she murmured, liking the feel and kissing him back. Then she pushed him away and in a mock stunned voice, said, "The first thing I want to know is, what happened to you? I was worried that you were hurt."

"I called, but there was no answer."

Julia frowned. "You must have called when I was next door seeing my neighbors. When I'm nearby I always leave the machine off."

"I had a flat tire." He looked at his hands, then grinned sheepishly. "I did my best with some towel wipes I had in the car, but they did nothing for my fingernails. Your dress–I hope I didn't leave smudges." He laughed. "Not that I care so much . . ." His eyes sparkled.

"I'll say." Her chuckle was full of affection. "I think I have some of that goop hand soap in the bathroom. Look in the basket inside the cabinet under the sink. I'm sure it's there," Julia said as she steered him in the right direction. She continued down the hall to the bedroom saying, "I'm going to do a quick change. I'll be ready in two shakes of a lamb's tail." Julia's heart sang as she searched her closet for a substitute outfit, selecting a pale blue sleeveless silk sheath with matching high heeled sandals.

Brad finished soaping away the grime from around his fingernails. While drying his hands he looked around, admiring the mauve and white decor with warm oak accessories that gave the room a Victorian look. Eyeing the squeeze-bottle of hand lotion on the top shelf of the wall *etageré*, he reached for it, nearly knocking over another bottle next to the lotion. Brad's eyes narrowed as he stared at the after-shave lotion in the glass bottle. The popular brand was one that he had used in the past. Frowning at it, he picked it up.

He'd known women to use the complementing cologne, but not the after-shave. He couldn't imagine the feminine Julia considering wearing the heavy woodsy scent. As he reached for a familiar-looking nut-brown leather case that was on the top shelf, his eyes darkened. Taking it down, he held the case for a long moment, staring at it as if at any moment it would ignite in his hands. "Dear God," he breathed as he lifted the lid. "Let it be empty." As he feared, nestled in the soft brown suede was a man's electric shaver. Beside it was a well-used styptic pencil. Not general feminine toilette stuff, Brad thought, snapping the case shut. Slowly he sat down on the flat edge of the bathtub, closing his eyes. His hand trembled as he rubbed his forehead, then massaged his throbbing temples. His lips quivered, so he clenched them together. He sought to quiet his boiling blood, which he imagined to be the red spots floating behind his closed lids. He opened his eyes to find he was still clutching the case. Moving slowly, Brad stood up, setting the case back in its place on the *etageré*. Suddenly, he reached out both his hands and grabbed the edge of the sink, gripping so hard the skin of his knuckles was stretched taut. The image of Jim Anderson holding Julia's arm danced before his eyes. He held on until the shaking in his body subsided and the sick feeling in his stomach left him.

He removed a paper cup from the holder and rinsed his mouth with the cool, mint green mouthwash. He doused cold water on his face and dried off with the soft guest towel. "Steady, man," Brad told himself. "After all–she is a beautiful woman–and beautiful women, it appears, simply cannot help themselves."

He glanced at his dark image in the mirror, smiling wryly. "Beauty and the Beast. Seems that's the story of my life," he thought. "Well, not my life–not this time–not ever again. This beauty will have to find herself a new game player." His shoulders set, Brad walked down the short hallway to the living room.

When Julia heard Brad leave the bathroom she, went to the kitchen and began putting ice in two glasses. She thought he might want a cold drink before leaving. Alcohol was out, knowing Brad left it alone when he drove. After pouring a Pepsi for him and white wine for herself, she returned to the living room.

As feminine as her bedroom was, Julia's living room was quite the opposite: hardwood floors, inexpensive rugs, deep comfortable sofa and chairs, it was a room to be lived in. She saw Brad sitting in one of the overstuffed chairs by the large picture window. He sat, leg crossed, methodically swinging his foot. His hands rested on each arm.

"Brad?" Her voice was a question. "What is it?" Julia's heart quickened as she set the glasses on the table, starting to walk towards him. She stopped as he lifted his eyes to her. "Brad," she whispered, frightened at the cold fury she saw in his eyes. Rooted where she stood, she could only stare, waiting for him to speak.

His eyes flitted to the glasses then back to hers. His mouth twisted wryly as he said in a cold and distant voice, "Cocktails before dinner?"

The familiar words filtered to Julia's brain but she remained unmoving, a sob beginning to catch in her throat. "I don't . . . Brad . . . what is it? I don't understand . . ." her voice failed.

Brad closed the space between them in two long strides, causing her to gasp at his sudden nearness. His voice was alarmingly soft. "You can stop the game, sweet Julia. You've won. I concede to you." He brought his hand slowly to his head in a smart salute, his smoldering eyes mocking. "Like all your kind, you play exceedingly well." He stepped back from her, allowing his gaze to slowly rake over her stiff body.

Julia, still frozen, felt her body go hot with shame for the insulting implication of his look. She started to speak but he quickly put a finger to her lips.

"Shhh. Don't speak. Don't say a word. I want to leave without hearing more lies coming from those exquisite lips. Shhh."

Though his voice was barely a whisper, Julia heard the hard controlled edge. Just as she backed away from him, he grabbed her hand. He held it tightly, fingering the tiny opal on her finger. He stared at it for a long moment then looked at Julia. The pain she saw in his eyes stabbed her heart. He had been wounded deeply. He stared coldly at her, as if etching her image in his brain. Then, turning on his heel, his gait measured, he walked toward the door. He unlocked it, but stopped as if he'd forgotten something. She watched as he turned to her, took something out of his pocket and tossed it on the foyer table.

Looking intently at her he said, gesturing toward the carelessly thrown object, "To the victor." He laughed, the harsh sound sending waves of hurt through her. "You know the rest." The hollow sound of his voice speared her as he disappeared.

The click of the door closing snapped Julia out of her immobilized state. She quickly walked to the door, locked it, leaning against it heavily. When her body stopped quivering she glanced at the shiny object that had landed in a tray of unopened mail. She picked it up, gaping at the work of art she held in her hands. The fire emanating from the deceptively tranquil stone brought a whispered sigh to her lips. She slipped the ring on her finger, the brilliant stone twinkling in its antique gold lace bed. She turned her hand, each twist causing yellow and blue fire to burn brightly in the core of the mysterious stone. Julia walked to the sofa where she sat, dazed, trying to make sense of the last half hour of her life.

Patiently she traced every minute from the time Brad walked into the apartment until the time she had found him sitting statue-like in the chair. She got up and traced Brad's movements, her cheeks growing hot when she thought of their fierce embraces on the couch. The last place I left him was in the bathroom. She entered the room and looked around. "Whatever it was, it started here," she told herself firmly. Puzzled, she looked around finding nothing out of place except the hand lotion. She reached for it, mechanically putting it back on the *etageré*, her hand nearly knocking over another bottle. Her gaze settled on the bottle of after-shave. "Oh, no," she gasped.

Julia picked up the leather case, opened it, then snapped it shut. "Oh, no," she said again, "Jim, Jim, Jim." She hurried from the bathroom, her crossed arms tightly hugging her heaving chest, "No, no, no." Her body shook. "It isn't fair. Brad thinks . . . oh, no." Her mind sped back to the scene on the street, Brad eyeing Jim so coldly. And now, she thought, the after-shave, the shaver. Julia's face was wet with tears though she made no sound. After what seemed like hours, she went to the kitchen where she took two aspirins, turned out the light and walked through the darkened apartment to her bedroom. Stepping out of her shoes she lay across the bed fully clothed, her arm flung across her forehead. She felt numb, except for the dull ache in her head. Her sad confusion and pain were slowly turning into cold fury. Brad actually thought Jim Anderson was the "someone else" in her life. Though she'd told him differently, in the end he chose not to believe her but rather, in his own mind, had drawn a conclusion based on the presence of two inanimate objects found on her bathroom *etageré*. She was becoming outraged that he had sought no explanation, but chose instead to automatically categorize her with those women in his life who meant less than nothing to him, women who had always been benefactors of his pretty baubles, and a “thank you” for a good time.

Sadly, Julia removed the opal from her finger. She stared at its light twinkling in the darkened room. “To the victor,” Brad had said. “No, my love” she whispered aloud. “You are wrong. So wrong.”

Chapter VIII

"Ms. Hart." Julia's eyes opened at the gentle pressure on her shoulder from the soft-voiced stewardess. "Fasten your seatbelt. We're landing in five minutes." Julia stared momentarily at the fresh-faced woman with the expressive dark brown eyes who waited to see that Julia was fully awake and fastening the belt before smiling and moving on to the next row.

Julia turned to look out of the plane window, only to be met with darkness and a million twinkling lights shining over the city of Paris. Her heart thumped wildly in her chest as she settled back, willing her body to move in sync with the plane's descent. She took deep swallows to prevent her eardrums from clogging with the pressure. Julia sighed at the first gentle bump of the wheels hitting the ground and the plane gliding to a smooth halt.

After what seemed like an interminably long time passing through customs, Julia frowned as she looked around. Her fellow passengers were retrieving their luggage, being greeted by friends and lovers and departing, while Julia had yet to spot Samantha. She finally commandeered the services of an airport employee, who stored her luggage on a cart. While moving towards the exit, eyes roaming for a glimpse of Sam's face, she spotted her name on a white cardboard held high in the air.

"Julia Hart" was printed in bold black letters. The young man dressed smartly in black chauffeur's garb looked inquiringly at Julia as she approached him.

"Ms. Hart?" he said in his thick Parisian accent.

"I'm Julia Hart."

He smiled, showing extraordinarily white even teeth, as he tipped his cap. He gestured to the luggage carrier and then led the way to his limousine.

"Ms. Sammí had a last minute engagement," he explained in an apologetic tone. "She said to please forgive her for not welcoming you to Paris. She will make every effort to join you as soon as possible."

Exhausted, Julia closed her eyes during the ride to Sammí's apartment. When she opened them, she was in downtown Paris. The chauffeur pulled onto the Champs Elysees and into the circular driveway of the beautiful George V Hotel. He removed Julia's bags and escorted her into the exquisite lobby where she was met by the hotel concierge. Amazed, Julia found that she was indeed registered for a week. During the ride up to the eighth floor, her thoughts were in a jumble. Sam knows I can't afford this place for one day, let alone one week, she thought in a daze. Feet sinking into soft gray mosaic carpeting, she followed the bellhop down the long hallway to her room. Once inside, Julia's mouth fell open in surprise. The room was a suite. From where she stood she could see that there were two bedrooms on either side of the spacious room. The decor was surprisingly elegant in pale pastels, the two sofas dominant in soft mauve. Julia walked to the round table in the living room and sniffed the huge floral arrangement.

She read the card. It was from Samantha. It read, "Hi, Ju. Please forgive me for not meeting you on your first trip to Paris. Isn't it beautiful? We're going to have a fantastic week together. I know you're complaining already about the expense. But this is my treat. This is one week you'll always remember. See you soon. Love, Sam."

Julia dropped to the comfortable sofa, still amazed, yet pleased. She smiled, her eyes filling as she thought about her sister's generosity. She was always one to see that others were being cared for, selflessly lending a hand whenever and wherever she could. Too excited to eat a full meal, yet hungry, Julia ordered room service. She requested chicken salad and a pot of tea. After eating, and tiring of waiting for Sam to return, Julia unpacked her bags and got ready for bed.

"Wake up, Ju," Sam was saying while pinching Julia's cheek. Somewhat awake, Julia reached up and hugged her sister. Samantha pulled the coverlet from Julia, took her hand and dragged her out of bed.

"Oh, no, you don't. You're not going to sleep away your first night in Paris without saying hello to me."

"Sam," groaned Julia, sleepily looking at the illuminated dials on the bedside clock radio. "I already have. It's nearly daybreak," she said. Then, "Where've you been?"

Julia donned her robe and arm-in-arm the two young women went into the living room, sitting side by side on the long sofa. Julia looked at her sister. Samantha was dressed in an ankle-length jade-green evening gown covered with shiny bugle beads. The dress was held up by twists of slim straps. She wore silver sandals and long dangling clear crystal and silver earrings.

"You look beautiful," Julia said. "You weren't working?"

"Yes and no," Samantha answered, kicking off her shoes and slipping out of her gown. She tossed on a white silk robe she'd been carrying when she woke Julia up. Tying the sash, she sat down again.

"We're never *not* working, even when we are supposed to be partying," she said, grinning at Julia. "It was one of those big society bashes where all of us models were supposed to make ourselves visible. But it was great fun. Many interesting people show up at these things." She eyed Julia curiously. Samantha neglected to say that among the interesting guests was one Bradford Coleman who was in the company of one the "beautiful women" of the Paris party scene.

When Brad had spotted Samantha, he extricated himself from the clutch of his date and started toward her. "Hi, little one," he said, giving her a kiss on her forehead. He seemed pleased to see her. "Brad," she said, showing her surprise at seeing him. "What brings you to Paris? I thought you were summering in New York with . . ." she had stopped before Julia's name escaped her lips. As if Brad knew what she was about to say, his eyes became like black ice as the smile left his lips. "Business," he said in clipped tones. Then, more softly, "I'm here on business, little one." They spoke briefly before he excused himself and returned to his companion. Samantha had stared after him for a long moment. She never mentioned to him that Julia had just arrived in Paris and was at that moment waiting for her at the hotel. From Brad's remarks, she knew that Julia's presence in the city was unknown to him. Ever since she had received the telegram from Julia a few days before, asking that she meet her flight, she'd mused about the situation.

After seeing Brad tonight, it didn't take a rocket scientist to fathom what had occurred. She'd been overjoyed at Julia coming and had set about to make it a trip she would never forget. Even before she guessed at the apparent reason for Julia's sudden change of heart about visiting, Samantha had engaged several of her friends to squire Julia around at occasions requiring an escort. Now that she was certain Julia was feeling some pain and misery, she was glad of her foresight.

"What are you looking so pleased about?" asked Julia, smiling at her grinning sister.

"Oh, nothing." Her eyes gleamed. "Have I got a week planned for you."

"Sam, I think you've done enough by renting this suite. It's expensive. What's wrong with us staying in your apartment?"

"Fiddlesticks. I'm tired of my apartment–besides, I'm being selfish. I don't intend for the two of us to spend precious time cooking and doing dishes. Here, we have the convenience of room service."

"But the expense?"

"Julia," Samantha's voice was firm. "Forget the expense. The suite is paid for. My treat. Don't worry about it." Putting a finger to her lips, she said, "No, not another word." Julia was about to protest.

With a sigh, Julia relented. "OK. But I'm going to pay my

share of our entertainment expenses. That's final," she emphasized when Samantha opened her mouth to protest.

"All right, Ju," Samantha said. She decided there was no need for Julia to know that several of the dinners and parties they would be attending were almost all complimentary or prearranged by Samantha.

With a yawn Samantha said, "Let's get some sleep now. We've a big day ahead of us. We're brunching at the hotel and later we'll start our shopping trip."

After chatting a bit about home and family, Samantha and Julia departed to separate bedrooms in the large suite.

As Julia's head hit the pillow, she immediately felt herself drifting into sleep. Her last thoughts were, "I'm in Paris at last. The eternal city for lovers. But I'm without my love."

* * *

"Samantha, my feet. They'll never be the same," moaned Julia. They were seated at a sidewalk cafe on the *Rive Gauche* where Sam, in French, ordered *salade verte, croque-monsieur* and red wine. Julia was impressed that Sam had mastered the French language. Julia said, "I understood the red wine, but what else did you order?" she asked.

"Oh, just a green salad and toasted ham and cheese sandwich," Sam replied airily. The girls laughed.

After shopping, Sam had taken Julia to the cafe via Gare d'Austerlitz since they had been walking and shopping all morning. Julia kicked off her shoes and tried to subtly massage each foot, while Samantha laughed.

"This is only the beginning, love."

"No. No more shops. I couldn't try on another thing."

"Not shopping, silly. Dancing."

"Dancing? Tonight?"

"Don't worry. We'll have your feet in fine shape by tonight. Paris discos are something to see. You'll love it. No escort needed. Everybody's everybody else's date. With that pink number you bought today you'll be a knockout. We'll be meeting some of my friends there."

"Sounds pretty much like a set-up to me," said Julia suspiciously. "You're not trying that old matchmaker stuff on me, I hope." She eyed her sister grimly.

"At a disco? No, Julia. Strictly fun, fun, fun. Don't worry. When I get ready to set you up, you're gonna know it."

They were silent for awhile as they ate. Julia tasted her red wine and stared at the late afternoon scene. Lunching at a sidewalk café on the Left Bank was one of the "musts" for tourists. The crowd was large and varied. Julia heard snatches of foreign languages. Looking about, she saw several tables with young women like herself and Samantha. Her eyes clouded briefly before she turned away. In the City of Love, with no love, she thought sadly.

After brunch at the hotel, she and Sam had visited one fashionable shop after the other. Sam had encouraged Julia to try on new styles and colors. "Time to wear some of the duds you've been selecting for your models," she said.

"You know my taste, Sam. Comfort."

"Ahh, but in Paris you must live a little." Sam's accent was French. She had insisted that Julia buy a hot-pink, slim, off-shoulder minidress that hugged her figure like a soft web. "You are crazy, darling, if you leave that dress in the shop," the salesman scolded. They purchased long earrings that reached her shoulders, and sandals in the same shade. Their shopping spree continued in designer shops where they purchased several outfits. Sam reached over and squeezed Julia's hand. "Thanks, Ju. I'm glad you're here. It's like I dreamed–you and I together in Paris."

Julia smiled at her sister, remaining silent. She was thinking of her reason for being in Paris and the thought brought a far-away look into her eyes.

"Want to talk about it?'

The soft voice broke into Julia's reveries. She looked at Sam, not bothering to try to hide her pain. "You never could be fooled, Sam."

Samantha shook her head.

"He just walked out, Sam. Just like that," Julia said, snapping her fingers.

Samantha remained silent.

"Sam, we were having a great time, enjoying one another–being together. We were inseparable for days. We laughed. We danced. We picnicked. We even went antiquing. Then . . ." her voice faltered.

Samantha gently nudged her hand, urging her to continue.

Julia looked at Sam, her eyes full of utter disbelief. "He walked out. We were going out to dinner. He came to my apartment. He saw Jim's shaver in the bathroom. Sam, the things he said to me. Hateful things . . . he was furious."

"What things?" prompted Samantha. Her eyes narrowed at the thought of anyone, including Brad, intentionally hurting Julia.

"I can't remember everything exactly, but–that because I was beautiful–that I was just doing what I was supposed to do, that I play the game well . . ." Julia's voice trailed away, full of hurt and bewilderment. Her eyes flickered with the memory. "Sam, he's hurting inside. Oh, not from his business mess–or even me. I believe it's something in his life that's haunting him." She looked away for a moment, then faced her sister again. "Your friendship with him . . . has he ever said anything, mentioned . . . another woman?"

"No. He's never talked about his private affairs. I don't know of any one special woman in his life. Not until . . ." she stopped when Julia stared at her curiously. "You, Julia," she continued. "You. The last time I saw Brad, there's no way that anyone could not tell me that he'd fallen for you like Humpty Dumpty fell off that wall."

Julia listened to her sister's words, nodding in agreement. She remembered the day he picked her up at the airport. The day they made love. Pursing her lips and shaking her head in a defiant gesture, she adamantly refused to believe that for him that day and the ones following were only ways to pass time with a new distraction. She said, "Sam, was his a happy marriage?"

"I'm not sure. I've never heard any gossip about it. I've never asked about his marriage," Sam answered, her face puckered into a frown. "Haven't you two ever talked about it?"

"Yes. Once. He only said that he'd been married."

"I've heard talk of him having a close friend in New York. But how close, I don't know. If you're really interested in his background, you know where to find it. I'm sure *Who's Who* can give you every little detail there is."

Julia summoned the waiter to freshen their drinks, thinking, Sam's right, of course, but I will not pry into Brad's life. Her eyes misted. As far as he's concerned, I'm nothing to him. If he ever decides that he was wrong, that he wishes to explain his behavior to me, then he'll have to seek me out, Julia thought. Until then, the Bradford Coleman that I knew for a few glorious weeks will have to remain but a memory. It's time I got on with my life. A small smile played about her mouth.

"What's so funny," her sister's voice interrupted her thoughts.

With a shrug of her shoulders, Julia smiled at Sam, saying, "No. I think I'll let sleeping dogs lie. I was thinking that if we don't hurry up and get married, our parents are going to adopt a kid and call it their first grandchild."

Samantha laughed, relieved to see Julia trying to chase away her gloomy spell. "I think you're right," she said with a grin. "With my new career and yours expanding, who has time for love, marriage and babies? Oh, no," she said in mock despair, "I'm afraid that for now they'll just have to call us the Hart spinsters."

They burst into laughter, each having her own vision of the Hart clan's reaction to them remaining unmarried and childless.

As if they had had the same thought, they spoke in unison, "No more family reunions for me."

After awhile, Sam began to gather their packages, saying, "Come on, sis. The Paris night awaits the scandalous Lady in Pink."

Brad poured the after-shave lotion into his hand and lathered it onto his face, grimacing at his image in the mirror as he did so. He smiled to himself wryly. Capping the bottle he stared at it. For days after leaving Julia's apartment, he couldn't handle his shaver or splash on lotion without anger welling up in his body like a ball of helium. But now, for the first time, he felt nothing. No anger. No remorse. No sadness. Just emptiness.

Surprising, he thought, arching a brow in self-mockery, it appears that a chance meeting with a Hart has had no deleterious effect. I must be cured, he mused, smiling sardonically at his dark image as he left the bathroom and headed to the phone. Wearing only a terry cloth wrap and barefoot, he propped himself on the arm of the sofa and dialed room service. After ordering a large breakfast, he proceeded to dress. When in Paris, Brad always made this hotel and this particular suite of rooms his home. He had tried several other hotels on previous visits but found that the personnel and service at the Warwick Hotel near the Champs Elysées best met his needs. They respected his need for privacy and were also very accommodating when he needed arrangements for impromptu meetings.

Dressed casually in a white shirt tucked into yellow and white checked pants, he stood nonchalantly at the terrace door, gazing over the city. The view from high above the teeming street below was spectacular on a clear day. Suddenly a troubled look appeared on his face. As if transported back in time, he was on another terrace in another city, but he was not alone: the perfumed scent, the tinkling laughter of a beautiful woman. The sound of the door chime caused the scene to dissipate, becoming part of the Paris smog. He shook his head–whether to clear the ghostly image or bring it back, he was not certain. He left the terrace to answer the repeated chime. He opened the door to the waiting bellman who had brought his breakfast.

The hot, aromatic dark liquid burned his throat as he swallowed too quickly. He had carried his breakfast tray to the terrace where he sat eating and looking over the notes he'd made since his arrival. His own investigation of David Jensen had turned up some interesting facts. Soon Brad became distracted, his thoughts drifting to his meeting with Samantha.

Not entirely surprised to see her at the gathering, he was pleased to see his young friend again. In her wise ways, she had stuck to generalities in their conversation, never uttering her sister's name. Brad could see she was surprised at his appearance, as if she expected him to still be in New York. But of course she would have had no way of knowing he planned to leave. He had never told Julia of his plans. He felt Samantha's eyes on his back as he returned to his companion and shrugged, knowing she was wondering about his relationship with her sister. She'll find out soon enough, he thought. He held no animosity towards the sweet, innocent Sammí. After all, she was not her sister's keeper.

With an effort, Brad turned back to his papers, frowning at the information he and a few select employees had gathered. Coupled with the information JJ had dug up on one David Jensen, Brad felt they were on to something. According to the extensive computer research done by Brad's own employees, David Jensen turned out to be a former employee of TAMA Corporation long before Brad had acquired his vast holdings. It appeared that Jensen had been around the fast food franchise business since he was a teenager working himself up to store manager. Though starting his career with a competitor, he had come to TAMA Corporation with vast supervisory experience, having managed several different stores during his career. His record showed that he excelled in start-ups, first-time stores in out-of-the-way areas. His ingenuity and aggressiveness had the new stores flourishing and turning a profit in record time; then abruptly Jensen had dropped from sight. There was no record of his being employed in the industry for at least three years. Curiously, he surfaced as one of the top executives in the employ of Brad's foremost competition. The same competition who opened their own first-time Paris store only months after Brad's grand opening.

Brad tossed the papers on the large coffee table and sat back on the sofa, wearily rubbing his eyes. With all the data, Brad had not a clue to what any of it meant and why JJ had zeroed in on this one man. He reasoned that both stores had opened successfully, were flourishing, had the normal spurts of ups and downs, and had competitive but friendly ad campaigns. Hardly anything vicious. He picked up the papers again, rifling through them. Disquieted, he threw them back on the table and muttered, "There's not one clue here from JJ as to why he singled out Jensen. He's not even the executive in charge of the Paris store—he's based in the New York office."

The intensity of Brad's grimace caused his temples to throb. In a swift move, he picked up the phone and punched the button for the operator.

"I'm placing a long distance call to New York," he replied to the operator's question. Hanging up after giving his information, he sat and waited for the operator to place his call.

"William, what the hell is JJ up to?" Brad exploded when he heard his attorney's voice.

"How's the weather, Brad?" William Brooks said, his voice smooth and unhurried.

"Damn it, William. I'm not calling transatlantic to tell you the sun is shining," he said, exasperation framing his face.

"Oh, the sun is shining? Be thankful. The heavens have opened up here for two days now. I just put in my order for a row-boat," he said, a chuckle in his throat.

Brad's grip on the phone loosened as his face lost some of its tension and his eyes began to twinkle. He sighed into the phone but said nothing, marvelling at his friend's technique for calming him down.

William, hearing Brad's sigh said, "Better?"

"Thanks, William. Better. You do it every time."

William laughed, "I'd better. I want you to keep sending those hefty checks our way."

"It's more than money, William, and you know it." Their friendship never had to be put into words. All through college and afterwards, they'd been there for one another. Lately, Brad thought, where he was concerned, William was working overtime.

"Yeah, I know," William said. Then, clearing his throat, he asked, "Run into a problem?"

"We're stumped. Nothing in JJ's notes tells me anything about any suspicious acts of wrongdoing on Jensen's part. No one has even seen him in Paris. Not one employee or manager on any of the shifts has ever seen him at the store, much less heard his name. Could JJ have missed something?"

"It's not like JJ to have been misled."

"But there's gotta be something . . . some clue . . . something so obvious we're missing it."

"You're probably right. Look, I'll get JJ in here and take everything from the top. Then I'll get back to you." He waited a moment, then slowly William said, "Brad . . . I suppose you want to get back here as soon as possible." He added, "Listen, there's no need for you to stay. If something new comes up, we can handle it."

"No," Brad replied brusquely. "No," he repeated, in a calmer voice. "I'm staying. There's nothing important for me to attend to in New York. I . . . I've finished my other business there," he ended firmly.

"I see," William said, a frown creasing his brow. The controlled anger in his friend's voice did not go unnoticed. "Well, then. I'll stay in touch."

Chapter IX

The pleasant laughter of the happy young group broke Julia's reverie. "Come on, Julia, 'fes up," said the handsome, dark-eyed young man seated beside her. His voice, while mellow, with a British sounding lilt, held a soft challenge. His walnut skin had turned browner under the torrid Paris sun. Julia knew that the 25-year-old Jeffrey had developed a crush on her.

"Yes, tell us, Julia," another deep male voice interrupted. "Tell this little pup here that it is Simon you have fallen in love with."

Julia threw her head back and laughed, her eyes twinkling. She looked around the table at the smiling faces of Samantha's friends, Simon, Jeffrey, Zeena and Patsy. They'd spent the morning together touring the Louvre and other art galleries and now, finishing lunch, they were headed for the Eiffel Tower. She'd met them only that morning, all but Jeffrey, whom she'd met at the disco her first night in Paris, and who seemed besotted with her. They were a diverse group. Sam was the only model and the youngest. Jeffrey and Zeena, who were twenty-five, were exchange students from England. Both were studying music. Patsy was a 30-year-old secretary with a diamond firm and Simon was a 32-year-old lawyer who'd returned to school to study art, his first love. Another friend,

Marietta, a dress designer and the only Paris native, had gone off somewhere with Sam.

Sam had felt comfortable about leaving Julia with her friends, knowing they'd see her back to the hotel safely, especially Jeffrey. As a matter of fact, Sam's parting words to Jeffrey had been, "I don't want to find you've kept Julia from dressing for her date tonight." Jeffrey had replied in a injured tone, "You will be sorry when I am found suffering from a broken heart. You will never forgive yourself." Samantha had departed, shaking an admonishing finger at him.

Julia felt happy. The last few days Sam had kept her on a merry-go-round, non-stop shopping, parks, museums. They'd even toured the rural areas, stopping at a roadside country inn where Julia had feasted on simple tasty fare. Though her hunger had been satisfied, she still could not resist sampling the scrumptious-looking desserts.

Before she and Sam had left the hotel that morning to meet the group, Sam had informed her of the party they would be attending later on in the evening at the fabulous Angelique Hotel. "Remember when I told you I'd let you know about setting you up?" Samantha had said, a gleam in her eye. Julia had looked at her sister warily, barely nodding her head. "Well, tonight's the night," Samantha had said, barely able to contain her excitement.

"What?"

"Tonight, your escort to this *very* fancy shindig is Henry Montgomery, the most eligible bachelor in town. You had better hold on to your pantyhose because the felines will be knocking you over to get to him."

"You're certainly enjoying yourself, young lady," Julia said. "What, pray tell, did you promise him and why ever did he accept?"

"Ahh. Trade secrets. You know the game. Tit for tat. He owes me one. He's not about to refuse me."

"If he's such a great catch, why's he still available? What makes him Mr. Eligible?" Before Sam could answer, she added, "Besides, I'm not interested in marrying a Frenchman and living in France, thank you. My career awaits."

"He's an American. Georgia born. He's wealthy, owns a diamond export business. Interested yet?"

Julia's eyes had narrowed. "Why aren't you?" she asked.

Samantha's giggles had filled the room. "Not my type. I think M'Dear and Dad would definitely draw the line at me bringing home a 'friend' nearly 40."

"Oh, you throw me to the dirty old man, is that it?" Julia had tossed a pillow at her sister.

Now, sitting here with Sam's exuberant friends, she smiled because, thanks to her sister, she had had no time for her thoughts to drift to *another* wealthy businessman.

Inside the cool café, across the room, Brad's back was to the window where the soft chattering group was sitting. He'd finished his lunch and sat smiling, listening to the pleasant sounds of young voices. Their problems seemed insurmountable to them, but were only little annoyances that Brad would trade gladly.

His hand froze, clutching the napkin he was about to toss onto the table. The clear musical sound of that laughter wrenched his heart. No, it could not be, he thought. His senses reeling, his breath caught in his throat. Hearing the laugh again, his eyes closed tightly, then opened to become dark narrow slits. How could she be here? Still seated, he turned slowly, his mouth thinned to a grim line as he stared at Julia. She's more beautiful than I remembered, he thought. He watched her interaction with the group. Clearly, she was popular, her company enjoyed by her companions. Especially by the lovesick youngster who couldn't keep his eyes off her. Brad smiled at that. But his eyes narrowed at the other man, an older one who seemed overly-attentive. Brad instantly dismissed him as he turned his gaze once again to Julia, whose satin sun-kissed skin gleamed warmly. Her dark eyes and lips smiled. She laughed at someone's comments. Her dark ringlets shone, glinting from the sun's rays piercing the window.

As he stared at her she suddenly became silent. A puzzled look clouded her face as her eyes began to roam the room. By the time her gaze reached him, Brad was standing, watching her, his expression closed, eyes shuttered. When her eyes locked with his, he slowly nodded his head in greeting, his mouth becoming a cruel slash.

Julia's face paled and she gasped in surprise. Her companions, concerned for her sudden change of mood, fearing she'd become ill, were solicitous. Her eyes never leaving Brad's, she murmured softly, apparently assuring her friends that she was fine. He saw her stuff her hands in her lap, balling them into tiny fists.

He reached their table. Acknowledging her companions with a slight incline of his head, he focused his unfathomable stare on her, thinking, Damn, what will it take to rid this woman from my system? He stood close enough to her to get a whiff of her perfumed skin, and the scent of jasmine brought back memories of when he'd held her tightly in his arms aboard an old paddle wheeler. Julia, why do you haunt me?

Aloud, he said, "*Mademoiselle*," a smile barely playing across his lips.

Julia, moving as if in a dream, pushed her chair back and stood facing Brad, wondering if she could sit back down before her shaking legs embarrassed her. She willed her hand to behave as she extended it to him. She wanted to touch him, to caress his face, to gently trace the sarcastic smile on his lips.

With arched brow, Brad glanced at her proffered hand. He took it, brought it slowly to his lips, pressing his mouth firmly against it. "*Mademoiselle*," he repeated.

Julia's cheeks flamed hotly at his actions. Her table companions were unaware of the mockery behind Brad's French greeting to her.

"Brad." Her voice was a soft whisper. She could say no more, but stood waiting. She thought how cruel fate was. She longed to have Brad at her side laughing with her, loving her in Paris. Now, when she had not thought of him in days, closing her heart to him, he appeared before her in the most nondescript of cafés in all of Paris. She shook her head in utter disbelief, unwilling to acknowledge that familiar sensation warming her body to its core. "Brad," she repeated, finally finding her voice. "How are you?" she asked, her voice getting firmer with each word. She bit her lip. Mundane cafe, mundane question, she thought stupidly.

As though reading her mind, Brad allowed a smile to touch his lips briefly as he replied, "I'm fine, Julia. I see you've finally made it to Paris. Anyone . . . uh, any reason in particular . . . other than visiting your famous sister, of course?" he ended, his eyes filled with sarcasm, but his face deceptively pleasant.

"No. Nothing special. Other than fulfilling my dream of visiting this splendid city. It's really quite beautiful . . . I'm sorry it's taken me this long to experience it," her answering look and impersonal tone matching his. So, Julia thought, if this is the way you want to play it, I'm game. Aloud, she said, her voice searching, "And you?"

Brad's lifted brow showed surprise and his eyes shone with amusement at Julia's sudden attack. His mirth turned to admiration at her quick recovery for he knew she was stunned at their meeting.

"Business," he murmured. "Business, as always." He was still holding her hand and now glanced at it for his fingers failed to feel the tiny opal ring she always wore. Her fingers were devoid of all jewelry. Smiling quizzically, he decided she'd lost her penchant for opals.

Julia pulled her hand free, saying, "Nice running into you, Brad, but I really must leave. We've made plans and it's growing late. Maybe we'll meet again soon." The smile on her lips never reached her eyes as she turned away.

Brad's scowl deepened as he watched her leave with her friends. Within moments they disappeared among the throngs of shoppers and tourists. He stood outside, leaning against the red-brick wall of the café, hands thrust deep into his pockets, looking darkly at the scene before him. His stomach churned. He waited, struggling to regain control of his emotions. The chance meeting with Julia had triggered all his turbulent feelings of their last time together. He had simultaneously wanted to hold her, make love to her and to cause her pain. Wearily, he pushed himself away from the building and began to walk the several blocks to his hotel, unmindful of anything but his last glimpse of Julia.

A few blocks away, Julia turned to her new friends and said, "Would you mind if I called it a day? I think I'd better rest a bit before tonight." She laughed good-naturedly. "If I back out of tonight, Sam would never forgive me." As they all began to protest, Jeffrey, who'd intently studied the exchange between Julia and Brad, now held up his hand, saying, "No, no. Julia's right. You all know our Sammí." To Julia he said, his warm brown eyes serious,

"Would you like me to ride to the hotel with you, Julia?"

Julia looked intently at Jeffrey, surprised. Inwardly, she thought, Our little pup is not so young after all. She smiled at him, her eyes acknowledging his understanding. "Thanks, no, Jeffrey. But I'd appreciate it if you would help me land a taxi."

Once inside the car, waving to them as the taxi swung crazily into the flow of traffic, she settled back, her mind spinning wildly over her plan. She said aloud, "I'm sorry, Henry Montgomery, but tonight will not belong to you." She laughed, her eyes twinkling as the driver half-turned to look at her, muttering something like "Ah, American."

Brad slammed the phone down for the fourth time since he had arrived back at his hotel. The first call he'd made was to Samantha's apartment. He got her service, who refused to give any information on her whereabouts. He finally left a message that she return his call. The next three numbers he called were to hotels looking for a Ms. Julia Hart. The phone rang and he sprang to it ,hoping it was Samantha. "Hello," he said, trying to keep his voice under control.

"Darling," the well-modulated voice cooed. "You sound so breathless. Are you running?"

"Damn," muttered Brad at the sound of the unexpected voice. "What is it, Rita?" he barked into the phone.

"Darling."

The injured tone went completely ignored by Brad.

"If you are fighting with someone, please don't take it out on me. I'm only calling to remind you of the time you're picking me up tonight, darling."

"I know what time I'm picking you up tonight, Rita. I'll be there," Brad said rudely, hanging up on her next word.

Almost immediately he picked up the phone again, dialing Samantha's number. Upon hearing the service operator, he swore, hanging up without a word. He went to the terrace and stared out at the sun-drenched city. "I'll find you, Julia," he said to the breeze. "Soon, I'll find you. We'll continue your little game. Why not? I'm crazy for wanting you near me. But," his eyes were hard, "one thing you'll never hear in this dangerous game we play . . . is that . . . I love you, Julia. I love you so damned much."

Julia left the beauty salon and went to the hotel *parfumérie*. She found what she wanted and left with her purchases, leaving her wallet a tad lighter. A smile appeared. She was thinking that she should have used her "plastic," since tonight could bring many surprises and some "mad money" might be useful. When she entered the suite, Samantha was in the living room. Idly watching a news program while sipping a glass of white wine, she looked inquisitively at Julia, who dropped her purchases on the table and sat down beside her.

Samantha quickly decided that she'd say nothing about Brad's call, which she had not returned.

Neither sister spoke as they looked at one another, both pairs of eyes full of questions.

Samantha broke the silence. Picking up her glass she stated, "You know."

Julia nodded. "How long have you known?"

"Since the night you arrived. He was a guest at the party." When Julia remained silent, Samantha continued. "From his conversation, I gathered he didn't know you were here. I also guessed that you and he were . . . no longer friends." Samantha shrugged, "So I said nothing." She took a long sip of the wine, sat the glass on the table, turned to Julia and said, her voice and eyes full of concern, "What happened, Ju?"

Julia's eyes blazed. "In the days that followed, you still said nothing." She ignored Samantha's question.

Samantha shrugged again. "I thought that whatever had happened between you two, if you were meant to get together, you'd do it without my interference." An impish grin crossed her face. Spreading her hands in a gesture of helplessness, she said, "See? It's happened."

Julia laughed at her sister. One never stayed peeved with the lively Samantha for very long. She finally answered Sam's question. She described the meeting in the café, how Brad had been cool and distant, how she'd felt at his obvious intent to hurt her. She explained to Sam that in a flash her whole demeanor towards Brad changed as if she suddenly had become a chameleon. With her expression, her tone, her words, she had let Brad know–the war was on.

"What?' Samantha's voice sounded incredulous.

"Sam," Julia continued, "in a flash I realized that I was still hurting and trying valiantly to hide my feelings. I acted as if I had thrown a veil over my life. I also realized that the man I loved was standing before me, full of hurt, pretending for all the world to see that he couldn't give less than a good damn about me." Julia's eyes blazed with the memory. She looked intently at Samantha. Her eyes began to soften as she spoke. "I made my decision then, that only one of us will continue playing the injured lover and it's not going to be me. I'm ending it tonight," she stated, her eyes now gleaming with excitement.

Samantha caught Julia's infectious mood. Exasperated with impatience, she said, "What are you talking about? What are you planning, Julia Hart?"

"The seduction of Bradford Coleman."

"Oh, my God, no," exclaimed Samantha, slapping her forehead. "What have I created?" she groaned.

"Not what you've created, sister dear. Blame it on Paris if you will. The City of Lights . . . romance . . . making love."

"But tonight. Your date with Henry Montgomery. And Brad . . . where are you meeting him?"

"I'm afraid poor Henry will find he's just my escort tonight. Once we're there, I'm sure he'll become quite occupied. I'll find Brad, I'm sure."

Samantha looked at her sister quizzically. Though full of questions, she asked simply, "How do you know Brad will be there tonight?"

"I just know," Julia replied. When Samantha said nothing, but looked puzzled, Julia said, "You said yourself, the '*Who's Who*' of Paris will be there tonight." A smile crossed her pretty features. "I expect to see Brad."

"Julia?"

"Yes?"

"You're not setting yourself up for a big hurt, are you?'

For a moment, Julia was quiet. "Don't worry about me, Sam. I'm not unbalanced." Julia patted her sister's cheek. "I only want to spend the rest of my time in Paris with the man I love. If by the time I'm ready to leave he still can't bring himself to admit he loves me . . ." she shrugged, "then I'll go home and get on with my life." Leaning over, she tweaked her sister's ear. "Trust me, small fry."

"Ju, no matter what happens I will still keep him as my friend. We have that kind of relationship."

Julia smiled, "I know, Sam. Friends are not to be discarded. Especially on the whims of others. Be friends with him. Always."

Sam reached over and kissed her sister's cheek. "Good luck, Ju. Oh, I just want you to know that I'll be staying at my place tonight. I sort of have a date tonight myself." She broke out of her sister's grasp as Julia began to tickle her unmercifully.

Julia surveyed herself in the wall mirror of her bedroom in the suite. Satisfied with what she saw, she prepared to go meet Henry Montgomery, who was in the living room. He'd arrived only moments after Samantha's date and all three were awaiting her entrance. Twisting about, checking all angles, she could find nothing out of place. She opened a drawer, removed the opal ring from the lace hanky and slipped it on her ring finger. The brilliant gemstone shimmered in the soft light. Her eyes clouded just for a second, then cleared as she stared at the beautiful stone. Since she had picked it up off her foyer table in New York, she always kept it with her.

Her freshly trimmed and shampooed cap of black curls glistened with ebony lights; the black ankle-length crepe gown she'd chosen accentuated her generous bustline and slender waist, the gathered halter-top parted in the center to gently wrap each breast, leaving the rest of Julia's tawny beige skin bare. The Empire waistline was high, meeting the halter just under the breasts and soft filmy chiffon puffed at either hip, cascading past the hemline. A tiny jewel sparkled on each black silk, high-heeled sandal. Earrings that reached her shoulders glittered with the colors of the rainbow when the iridescent stones caught the light. She reached for the expensive bottle of perfume she'd purchased earlier and put a final dab behind each ear. Wearing the delicious creation, a Lapidus scent, would do wonders for her confidence, she knew. Julia then left the bedroom, closing the door softly and entered the living room to meet her date.

Though the two couples left the suite together, they rode in separate limousines to the Angelique. Henry and Julia's limousine reached the driveway first. They waited for Sammí and her escort to leave their limousine before entering. As soon as Sammí appeared, the onlookers murmured their recognition and appreciation of the beautiful young model. As they entered the glittering grand ballroom, murmurs went up in a crescendo, causing the guests to look to see who was creating the stir.

"Oh, I see Sammí has arrived, drawing a crowd as usual. Whew! But who is that lovely creature with Henry? My, my, my!"

Brad turned lazily toward the small crowd that had surrounded Sammí. His eyes softened when he spotted her, though he'd been annoyed that she hadn't returned his call. She was gorgeous in her knockout red ankle-length-gown. But he wondered who his date, Rita Smith, was going on about.

The crowd shifted, allowing him to see Henry Montgomery and the beautiful woman on his arm. "Julia!" Her name escaped his lips as though he spat out bitter herbs.

Rita Smith looked at Brad with arched brows. "Brad, darling, do you know the creature?"

"The 'creature', Rita, is Sammí's sister, Julia . . . and yes . . . we've met," Brad scowled angrily as the little entourage headed their way.

Sammí had spotted him and waved while starting toward him. Brad waved back and waited, jealousy rolling over him like a tidal wave as he stared dangerously at Henry Montgomery. "If you think you've caught the brass ring, fellah, you'd better think again," Brad muttered under his breath. His narrowed eyes moved to Julia. The sight of her rendered him breathless. She was a walking dream.

Apparently he wasn't the only male in the room thinking so. Her group of admiring suitors grew larger than Sammí's, much to Montgomery's dismay and Brad's malicious satisfaction. Julia smiled demurely at each admirer, murmuring whatever niceties people murmur at such times, Brad supposed. But when her eyes found his, they never left, not even when Henry whispered in her ear. She only smiled, nodded her head, murmuring something back, her eyes still locked with Brad's. She was sending a message to him and hardly being obtuse; he caught every signal. By the time they reached Brad and Rita, Brad's eyes had filled with sardonic mirth. He thought, "So that's the game we're playing tonight." His nod was imperceptible to all but Julia as she allowed a smile to play about her lips. Oh, Henry, you poor fool, Brad thought, you don't know what's about to hit you. A chuckle escaped his lips as he shook his head at this turn of events.

"Hello, Brad," Samantha said.

"Hello, yourself," Brad said, a reproving look in his eye.

"I know. Your message. Well, would you believe for the first time in my life, I was speechless," she grinned impishly. "So I thought Julia would explain much better than I. You remember my sister, Brad?" she said turning to Julia.

Brad looked at Julia. His eyes expressionless, he nodded, murmuring, "Julia."

Julia turned to him smiling sweetly. "Hello, Brad." Her eyes were veiled.

"This is my sister's first visit to Paris, Brad," Samantha was saying, catching his attention. "I'm sure you'd like to hear all about her impression of our adopted city." Talking non-stop while turning to Julia, she said, "Wouldn't he, Ju? I'll keep Henry company for you. You don't mind do you, hon?" she said as she put her arm through the surprised bachelor's arm, leading him and her own date away, her entourage following. Samantha, still chattering, turned her head, winked at Brad and Julia as she was swallowed up in the crowd. Brad's date, Rita, who had spied an admirer, drifted away.

Brad threw back his head and laughed, the sound coming from his gut, his eyes twinkling merrily. "Why, that little minx. Has she been studying acting secretly?" He laughed again; this time Julia joined him, causing him to turn to her. "Your idea?" he asked, his eyes filling with a mixture of admiration and disdain.

"No. I'm afraid not. Our little Sammí's got a bag of tricks all her own."

"Family trait?"

Julia tensed, the smile leaving her face, but only momentarily. He's not going to ruin my plan, she thought. She smiled seductively. Beneath lowered lashes she said, "You might say that."

"Then how about showing me some more of yours. Maybe

something along these lines." In one fluid motion, Brad cupped Julia's chin in his hand, bringing her lips to meet his in a swift savage kiss, his tongue reaching deep into her mouth.

Startled, Julia began to pull away, but almost immediately regained control. Relaxing, she allowed her body to go soft. She began to return Brad's kiss, her tongue becoming the aggressor.

A warm glow sped through his body. Abruptly, Brad jerked back as if brushed by blue flames. His movement caused Julia to sway off balance but he quickly caught her before she stumbled.

The feel of her bare skin sent shocks of electricity coursing through him at lightening speed. The look he gave her was filled with surprise and grudging admiration at her cool display of confidence. He took her elbow, leading her through the crowded ballroom. "A quiet little corner will do us fine right now," he said in a ragged whisper.

"I like it fine."

"What?" His voice was a scowl.

"Our private little corner. It's perfect."

Julia was pleased. Brad had guided them to the hotel's elegant cocktail lounge. Except for the long oval bar filling the middle of the room, almost every table was situated so that each appeared to be in a corner of its own. The light was soft and the red upholstered arm chairs soft and deep. They sat across from one another tasting their drinks, each eyeing the other. Julia had ordered a twist of lime with her gin and tonic and now squeezed the lime, discarding it on her napkin.

Brad sipped his Hennessy, staring thoughtfully at Julia. He sat his glass down, then reached slowly for her hand. She said nothing when he picked it up in his. He ran his finger gently over the shimmering opal stone, caressing it, a mysterious smile appearing on his lips. A faraway look flickered fleetingly in his eyes and was gone, as if some memory was too painful to linger. He lifted his eyes to hers, still holding her hand.

Julia watched Brad intently. The look on his face wrenched her soul. "It's so beautiful," she whispered. "So beautiful."

At the sound of her voice, Brad slowly let go of her hand. "What are we doing to one another? Can you tell me?" His low husky voice was barely audible.

Julia remained silent. To speak now, with the tears swelling her throat, would prove disastrous. She intended to stay strong through this contest she had started. A contest with no losers . . . or winners. A contest where two people would only find each other.

Brad, failing to see her struggling with her emotions, sat back, his eyes darkening. Taking her silence for shallow disinterest in his sudden display of emotions, he cruelly asked, "You've heard Paris is a better playground?"

Anger flashed across Julia's face. Her eyes blazing, she retorted, displaying her hand, "Yes," she hissed. "If this can be gotten in New York, then what, pray tell, will Paris bring?" She stood up, trying to escape before the tears behind her lashes spilled onto her cheeks. She cried to herself, I can't continue this. It's too painful.

Brad caught her, guiding her back to her seat. "Julia, look at me. Please. That was a rotten thing for me to say. I'm sorry. Forgive me. Please."

Slowly, Julia nodded. She smiled at the white handkerchief he handed her. "I remember another time I needed this," her voice a shy whisper, handing him back the cloth after wiping her eyes.

Brad's eyes softened. "I remember too." After a moment he said, "I'm glad you've decided to visit Samantha before she leaves Paris. She's always talked about the fun you two would have together."

Though she remained silent, he could feel the tension between them begin to melt. Rather than voice his curiosity as to how and why she was really sitting before him, he asked instead, "Is she meeting your expectations?"

"She?"

"Gay Paree." He lifted both hands palms up and shrugged. His voice took on the pose of a Griot as he continued in a pronounced French accent. "Many come, expecting much. To live their dreams. Yet . . . they of the false hearts . . . leave disillusioned. Angry, hurt, they blame her." His mouth moved in a sad smile. ". . . and poor Paree?. . . She becomes sad. So . . . she accepts the pain, . . . ahhh, but only momentarily. For she knows that soon, when she is twinkling in all her splendor, there will come those whose hearts are true. They will have fallen under her magical spell. They will leave, hearts filled with song and joy. And Paree? She basks in their happiness."

Julia looked at Brad intently when he ended his tale. She could read nothing in those veiled eyes. He stared back at her, unmoving except for the silent circular motion he made with his glass, turning it around and around on the polished wood surface of the table. Sadly, she realized the truth. That Brad would never toss away that veil of hurt he wore, never expose his bruised heart again. Unwilling to accept defeat in her renewed quest, she asked, "And what of the others?"

"Others?"

"They of the false heart."

Brad quirked an eyebrow. Was she really listening, he wondered. A smile played about his mouth. He felt compelled to continue his tale, his voice no longer affected, his eyes boring into hers. He continued, "They continue to travel from beautiful city to magical city, hoping, seeking . . . never staying long . . . but leaving empty and alone. Yet, always, the city that was left behind is blamed for their disillusionment. They never look unto themselves for the cause of their pain." Brad's eyes flickered briefly as he gave a short laugh. "But," he continued, "the cities survive. The vast number of true hearts are, as they say, legion."

"I believe that," Julia murmured softly.

As swiftly as Brad's mood had darkened, it brightened. "I'd better get you back to the party. I'm afraid I've monopolized you. Poor Henry must be frantic," he said, a big grin appearing on his face.

Brad helped her to her feet. Julia smiled. "I'm sure he never noticed. But I do want to say goodnight to him," she said as they left the lounge. "And what of your date? You were with someone?" her voice hung in the air.

Eyeing her steadily, not missing the unasked question, he answered, "Yes. I escorted Rita. But Rita does not expect me to escort her home. See?" He nodded his head to a cluster of men. In their midst was Rita, holding court. The raven-haired beauty was dazzling as she attentively bestowed each suitor with an infectious smile and a 'darling.' Brad chuckled. "Rita hardly ever leaves with her escort. It's a thing she has. Something about maintaining her image."

Julia looked at the gorgeous woman; her black luminous eyes shone in her pale ivory skin; the naturally long black lashes swept her high cheekbones.

"A false heart," Julia murmured.

Brad glanced at her, but before he could speak, she said, her hand lightly touching his arm, "Brad. Would you take me home?"

He remained silent, regarding her thoughtfully.

"Samantha will make my apologies to Henry. I'll call her tomorrow to thank her." Then, answering the question in his eyes, she continued, "Sam's staying at her apartment tonight."

Neither Brad nor Julia spoke much during the drive back to the hotel. She was lost in thoughts of her own. When she'd begun the walk across the ballroom earlier, her steps bringing her closer to Brad, her cool, secure demeanor belied the storm inside that caused her heart to beat wildly.

He stood so majestically in his black cutaway and pristine white ruffled shirt. When he attentively spoke to the beautiful woman at his side, she felt a sheath of arrows pierce her heart. Momentarily, she had considered abandoning her plan, but had resolutely dismissed the thought. She was determined to be with the man she loved–and all else be damned.

Perhaps, she had thought sadly, whatever deep pain he harbored in the core of his soul, she could in some way help him to bear it. If only he would only open the door a little, allow her to step inside, she knew that it would only be a matter of time. Julia knew that she would have to be the initiator, for Brad's male pride would not allow it to be otherwise. She also realized the danger that lay in the plan. Brad would naturally take what was offered him, then brutally reject all else, feeling that his behavior was justified. She had shuddered with nervousness.

Head high, her message-filled eyes had locked with Brad's as she walked as confidently as she would have back at work conducting her weekly staff meetings.

Now she stole brief glances at his still profile, wondering what he could be thinking of her.

A smile appeared on Brad's lips as he pulled up to the hotel entrance, helping Julia out of the car, leaving the keys with the valet. He had felt the secret looks Julia had been giving him.

When he had seen Julia enter the room on the arm of Henry Montgomery, he determined then that he would be seeing her again before she left Paris. He never assumed that he'd be escorting her to her hotel. His thoughts were filled with curiosity and admiration for her skillful maneuvering. Whatever her aim, he was secretly pleased.

To be near her again, to touch her, to inhale her intoxicating perfume. When he had caught on, he decided to accommodate her, to let her continue her game of play, reminding himself that it was only a game. All games ended sooner or later with either a winner or a loser, depending upon how one looked at the results. He hoped that Julia would be as gracious in losing as she was in her pursuit of whatever it was she wanted of him.

During the ride up in the elevator he pulled her close to him, his arm around her trim waist. He felt her momentarily stiffen, then relax against him, a small sigh escaping her lips.

Chapter X

Unlocking the door with Julia's key, Brad guided her through and locked it. Without warning, Julia's stomach grumbled loudly. She groaned with embarrassment and her eyes flew to Brad's. Her eyes filled with warmth as he emitted a burst of laughter. Julia smiled and was soon laughing with him. Still chuckling, he led her through the opulent pastel living room, placed her on the sofa and reached for the phone on the console table.

"It never fails," he said, shaking his head in mock disbelief. "You're the only woman I know whose stomach wants equal time. Hunger? Is *that* the *only* emotion I raise in you?" He eyed her challengingly as he held the phone, giving her a quick wink.

While ordering cheese omelets, croissants and coffee, Brad kept his eyes on Julia for her approval.

She nodded her assent at his selections.

Hanging up the phone, Brad walked to the bar. "Same?" he asked.

At her nod, he fixed their drinks and headed back to the sofa, handing her a gin and tonic with a twist of lime. He took a sip of Hennessy, then sat the glass behind him on the sofa table.

Julia had slipped her shoes off and was sitting feet tucked under her, one arm resting on the back of the sofa. Her position caused the halter top to gap open, exposing a tantalizing portion of her bare breast.

The sight of her smooth satiny skin with the tawny glow brought back memories, making his throat dry. He took another sip of Hennessy, giving him a reason for using his hands. He wanted to touch her.

Unaware of his struggling emotions, Julia spoke. She asked about the various people she'd seen and met at the party–about Henry Montgomery and Rita Smith. She inquired about the progress being made by his attorney.

When their food was delivered they ate, continuing to talk amiably. They spoke about Julia's promotion, her excitement and her need to prove she could do the job as well as her predecessor.

Each was still as careful as they had been earlier in the evening not to mention their last heated meeting in New York.

Now, as they sipped the smooth blend of Swiss chocolate almond coffee, they sat eyeing one another.

Julia had once again tucked her feet beneath her.

Brad, jacketless, bow tie discarded, sat comfortably beside her, one arm and shoulder resting over the sofa back.

Both were silent. Content with the delicious food and their pleasant conversation, they were finally feeling relaxed with each other.

The cocktails, the coffee, enhanced their mellow mood. These last hours together seemed to make that stormy night in New York appear to be someone else's nightmare.

Julia stifled a yawn.

"Oh no," groaned Brad. "The abuse I take from this woman." He hit his forehead with a clenched fist. "After I satisfy her hunger she wants to fall asleep on me. Ye gods, woman. Think of my reputation."

Julia, smiling, reached out and put a finger to his lips, silencing him. She then leaned over and kissed his lips lightly. Leaning back and gazing at him intently she said, "Never abuse, my love. Never abuse."

Brad was stunned. The use of the endearment turned his body molten, the heat traveling from his tingling lips to his groin. He repositioned himself on the couch to shield the extent of his emotions.

Julia, startled at her choice of words, relaxed. She thought of their implication, but realized she had voiced what was in her heart. Whether the cocktails caused the reckless abandon or her bruised heart was the culprit, she didn't really care. Noticing Brad's discomfort at her choice of words, she thought, It's true, Brad. Meet me, please. She then reached out, placing her hand on his cheek, caressing it softly, her thumb gliding gently back and forth over his lips. Her feelings for him were revealed in her eyes.

His emotions swirling like wind-tossed tumbleweed, he caught her slender hand, capturing it against his lips. He kissed her palm, her fingers, her palm again, placing tiny kisses along her arm, inhaling the tantalizing scent of her. The faint fragrance of violets and hyacinth evoked memories of a silvery moonlit night eons ago. He enfolded her in his arms. She came willingly, stretching her legs down to the floor, flattening herself to his chest, her arms twined around his neck. His lips found hers, devouring them in a savage, hungry kiss.

The intensity of her response encouraged his tongue to continue its exploration in the sweet recesses of her mouth. His hand traveled from her neck to her shoulder, lingering before he sought her breast through the soft silk of her dress. Slipping his hand under the loose halter top, he gently kneaded the nipple until it was a pulsating peak throbbing beneath his probing fingers. Continuing his exploration of her shapely contours, his hand rested on her nylon-clad thighs. The heat emitting through the fabric nearly singed his fingers.

At Brad's touch, his kisses on her body, Julia ached with her need for him. She cried out when his hand left her breast. Her mounting desire for him was rendering her senseless. She quivered as his hand roamed over her body leaving dangerous trails of quicksilver. She reached down to remove her pantyhose. With Brad's help she slipped them off, exposing her heated flesh to his hand. His mouth recaptured hers while he continued caressing her smoldering body.

The exquisite pain of his touches caused Julia to moan as she clutched him possessively. She could not will her hands to stop their own explorations. She slipped her hand through his buttoned shirt. Finding the tiny nipple on his chest, she gently ran her fingers over it. His hot breath tickled her ear as she heard him whisper his need for her. All the desire that she was feeling she heard in his voice. She murmured, her mouth against his throat, "Yes, Brad. I want you too . . . please."

Hearing her voice, he lifted his head. His eyes searched hers as he called her name, his husky voice barely audible.

Julia stood up. She held her hand out to him. With his hand in hers, she led him to the darkened bedroom. She had begun to slip out of her dress when he stopped her.

"No. I want to look at you." Turning on the bedside lamp, he faced her. He lifted both her arms in the air where she held them while he reached down for the hem of her dress, lifting it up and over her head, letting it billow to the floor. He gasped at her lovely nakedness. With her help he unbuttoned his shirt letting it fall beside her dress. Kicking off one shoe and then the other, he slid out of his pants. Swiftly removing his briefs and socks he stood naked before her.

Gently he reached out to touch her, caressing her nipples. He let his hand slide down her smooth belly. When his fingers touched her moist, heated mound, she moaned, "Brad."

"My sweet . . ."

He lowered her down on the bed, easing himself on top of her. Arching with pleasure from the feel of her hot bare skin, he wanted to take her immediately. With superhuman control, he willed his body to be still. His long-held desire for her was beginning to explode in his loins, but he wanted to savor her, to fill his nostrils with her sweet scent, to know every inch of her body, to memorize its soft curves. He wanted her–and he would have her. He knew she wanted him. Through the heat of his own passion, he felt hers.

"God help me, I love this woman." His anguished confession was silent. Aloud, he said in answer to Julia's plea, "I know . . . soon . . ."

Then suddenly, Brad stopped, groaning. He started to reach to the floor for his pants.

Julia stiffened when Brad became still. "What . . ."

"In my pocket. I have to get . . ."

Understanding, Julia touched his arm and with a twist of her body she reached to the nightstand, pulled opened the drawer and removed a small packet which she handed to Brad. His eyes flickered briefly.

"I prayed you would be here tonight," she whispered. Then, "Why else would Sam leave me alone tonight?"

Brad reached up and turned out the light, removing the foil covering and tossing the wrapper to the floor. With a groan he crushed her to him, his lips buried in the hollow of her throat, "Come here, you devious woman." In the pale quiet shadows their love was unleashed.

Brad's mouth came down on Julia's in a crushing kiss. His hands moved at will, leaving fiery trails, causing Julia to quiver and wince at the delicious sensation. Her hands moved down his back reaching his buttocks, then pressed his hardness to her fiercely. The friction sent electric currents through her as she lifted her hips in response.

Her uncontrolled passion sent shock waves of pleasure through Brad and the burning sensation in his loins, no longer containable, erupted into fire as he parted her legs and entered her.

The hot flame engulfed Julia. Her body writhed rhythmically to his motion, arching to meet every deep thrust. Gasping her delight, she felt her love for him flow through her body.

At the same time, Brad's passion climbed the pinnacle, the rising crescendo exploding into a river of hot lava.

Sated, they lay spent for a brief moment before Brad, sighing deeply, moved easily to her side, careful to keep his weight from crushing her. He gathered her in the fold of his arm where she lay quietly. He could feel the rise and fall of her chest. His own heart was pounding loudly against her cheek.

She put her hand to his chest. Lifting her head, she looked at him. Teasingly she said, "After such a light workout, one would not think you were tired."

Brad caught the smile in her voice. "Light, huh?" He put his hand against her chest which was quieting down. "Ummm. The lady has recovered, I see. Can I assume another 'workout' is in order then?" His eyes gleamed with mischief.

Julia said "Oh, no . . ." but was quickly silenced as Brad covered her lips with his. She moaned as she felt his arousal. Feeling one arm leave her, she soon heard him fumbling with the drawer. Hearing the sound of the foil, she grinned when he muttered, "The lady is prepared."

She laughed as she ended his mumbling with a kiss. With a swift movement, Julia turned over, her lithe body now laying full atop him. She lowered herself until her soft moist opening pressed against his hardness. Moving her hips in a circular motion while caressing his nipples with her tongue, she smiled when he emitted a groan of pure pleasure. When he struggled to reverse their position in order to please her, she resisted, whispering, "No, love. Let me love you." Then guiding him into her, she quickened the rotation of her hips.

Brad responded with one long convulsive thrust, the shock of the heated current moving Julia's body in a glorious shudder. After a moment Julia slid to one side, one arm flung over his chest as she snuggled close to him.

Brad was overcome. What they had just experienced . . . the pleasure she'd given him . . . were these the actions of a game-playing cutie?

On an emotional high, Brad dipped his face, kissing the top of her head, then ran his hand through the tousled ringlets. Almost immediately, realizing his error, he stiffened, instantly feeling Julia's body tense. A long incredible moment of silence passed until finally he felt Julia's hand on his. She ran her hand back and forth in a soothing caress. She sighed one long, deep sigh. Her voice drowsy, he heard her murmur, "I think I've finally buried that ghost." After a moment her chest rose and fell steadily. Brad kissed the top of her head once again, closing his eyes. He swallowed to loosen the tightness in his throat.

Securing the sash on her white silk robe, Julia answered the knock at the door. The waiter rolled the food trolley into the living room at her directions and quickly left as noiselessly as he had come. She checked each chafing dish and finding everything in order, she poured herself a cup of coffee before going to awaken Brad.

"Good morning."

The cup nearly flew from her hands as she started at the sound of his voice. She turned to see him standing casually in the bedroom doorway, wearing nothing but the evening trousers from the night before. She said, "Good morning," finding it hard to keep her eyes off his chest. The memory of the taste of his nipples in her mouth excited her, causing her eyes to gleam.

Looking at her curiously, he asked, "Are you all right?" Pushing himself off the wall he started towards her. Reaching her, he bent to kiss her lips.

Julia responded with a light kiss, then backed away. "Coffee?" she asked, starting to pour a cup before he replied.

Taking the cup, he sat on the sofa.

Julia sat on the other love seat facing his, drawing her knees up and sipping the hot brew. The short-sleeve, knee-length robe exposed her flawless golden thigh. Her dark hair, damp from her recent shower, glistened above her freshly scrubbed face.

The faint scent of lilacs drifted toward Brad.

Unaware of the tantalizing picture she made and the effect she was having on Brad, she smiled at him. There was love in her eyes. "Breakfast?" Or . . ." Her voice ended in a whisper.

"Breakfast. Now . . ." Brad said, his voice raspy.

Brad looked longingly at Julia, but adamantly remained seated across from her. He had heard her invitation. Pouring more coffee for them, he returned to his seat. He looked at her, his eyes unreadable. He had been awake when Julia arose. When he hadn't stirred, he felt her lean over and kiss his bare shoulder before she left the room. The touch of her cool moist lips sent a delicious sensation spreading through his body. He restrained himself from going after her because he wanted to talk to her with a clear head. He heard her showering, and when the soft musical sound of her humming reached his ears, his heart tightened. He meant to confront her. He was not leaving her without a satisfactory explanation of her behavior. He admitted that he had been flattered and excited when he decided to be a willing partner to her careful plans for him. But after their lovemaking, her uncontrollable passion for him, the words she had spoken—he was determined to force her to reveal what she was about.

He had decided that he wanted no more of the game. The torture was too much. Another woman–but not Julia. No more.

As she sat across from him, waiting for him to speak, his eyes shuttered, he said in a controlled voice, "Last night. Do you remember any of last night?"

"Last night? I know we were both feeling mellow but how could I possibly forget last night?" The smile on her lips never reached her eyes because of the deadly serious voice gripping her heart. Oh, Brad, she cried silently in anguish, can't you see through this facade? Why won't you say you love me? I'm offering my love to you. You must trust in me.

"We shared something beautiful last night, " he began, his voice low and husky. "There's no denying that we . . ." he paused. His whisper octaves lower, he said in wonder, "We were connected."

Say it, Brad, she willed him silently. Say we were two people in love . . .

"Do you remember your words? Tell me what you were saying, what you were feeling," Brad's look became fierce, his eyes darkening as he stared intently at her. "I must know. Was it the cocktails? The aphrodisiac of the night in Paris? Your admirers?" His eyes smoldered as his voice choked on the last word.

Julia's heart sank when she heard the hint of jealousy. Her mind flew back to the male toiletries he'd discovered in her apartment. She tried hard not to let the tears that had suddenly appeared behind her lashes begin to fall. She had lost. Bitterly, she thought about her gamble. Whoever he needs to help him combat his fears, she realized she was not to be the one. She was filled with an overwhelming surge of sorrow that suddenly saddened her dark eyes, sorrow for what could have been. He's asking now what last night was all about, she thought. Should she tell him that she was playing for high stakes? All she wanted was his love . . . to hear the man she loved tell her that he loved her. . .

Emitting a deep sigh, she squared her shoulders. For fear of Brad thinking less of her than he had when they'd met again at the café, she resolved to play out the scenario until she left Paris. Think what he would, she'd always have her memories of her love in the magical city, the city of dreams.

Smiling gaily, she closed the distance between them, joining him on the sofa. She touched his lips with her fingers. "Shhh. So serious so early?" She laughed. "I was warned that Paris could make you lose your senses. The cocktails, the people–for once I was part of the crowd instead of looking at life through a lens. It was such fun. But," she said, lifting her long lashes, her eyes gazing into his, "though I remember . . . our . . . our being together, I can't for the life of me remember a single word I said." Her voice fell. "Was it very important?"

Brad froze. Watching Julia warily, he searched the depths of her eyes for a long moment. Finally, smiling coldly, he spoke. "No, my sweet," leaning over and kissing her lightly on her lips, "it was not very important."

He stood up, pulling her with him, his whole manner changing. He seemed gay. Holding her at arm"s length, a grin parted his lips. "Look at us wasting this gorgeous day. What do you say I show you what this town's got during the daylight? You'll see some sights I'll bet Sam's never seen. Game?" He eyed her closely.

"Sure. Why not?" She ducked her head to hide her pain. "I'm certain it will be a memorable day," she ended softly.

Bending down and kissing her forehead, he said, "I won't be long," giving her a conspiratorial wink as he headed for the bathroom.

When she heard the door shut and the sound of the shower, Julia walked toward the bedroom to dress. The tears she had been holding back flowed slowly down her cheeks.

"Why do we deny ourselves?" Julia said in a soft voice. "We do. All the time." In answer to Brad's inquiring look, she said, "People. You, me. Everyone does it." Extending her hands in an expansive gesture to include the interior of the beautiful cathedral, she said, "This should be my second, third visit here. Not my first. I simply denied myself this experience. It's just so beautiful, Brad." Julia's hand was in his, and now she squeezed it tightly.

They sat quietly taking in the splendor of the ancient colorful edifice, the Church of St. Severin. The stained glass windows high in the ceiling glinted from the sharp rays of sun. It was late afternoon.

After leaving her hotel in the morning, they had stopped briefly at Brad's where he changed. Brad had then driven them out of the city to the small, historic village of Dix-Septieme. After walking about the fascinating sections of the curious town, its streets connected by a series of steep flights of steps, they stopped to eat. Lunch was at A'La Pomponnette, where the home-style cooking was favored by townspeople and tourists alike. They both had duck grilled and served with sauteed potatoes and huge green salads. Julia couldn't resist the dessert of baked *meringué* with ice cream, whipped cream and fruit. Before long they headed back to the city, Brad racing before the visiting hours ended at St. Severin. Making it in time, he proceeded to give Julia his own personal tour.

They sat quietly under the spell of the revered halls, hands still clasped.

"It is haunting. It's also a different experience . . . sharing it with someone else." Brad's voice was hushed. He stared straight ahead at the altar, though he felt Julia's gaze on his face. "I discovered this place the year before the business opened," Brad continued, speaking in a low voice. "The peacefulness that engulfs you is incredible. During the ups and downs of the planning stage, a visit here would miraculously clear the cobwebs away." He looked at her. "Before now, I've always come alone."

"Thanks for sharing. It's magnificent." Then, as if she had drifted to a distance place, she murmured, "Maybe I'll find a place of my own to return to when I visit again."

"Returning?"

"Yes. One day I will. One day."

She sat silently beside Brad watching him drive expertly through the madness of Paris traffic. He was accompanying her back to her hotel and then on to Sam's apartment. Before she and Brad had left in the morning she had called Sam. Since they had decided to check out a day early, Sam had agreed to pack their clothes while Julia spent the day with Brad. She had smiled at her sister's insistence. Sam would not listen to Julia's protests, claiming that her friend Mariette would help her. Julia was not to worry about a thing. The only things she'd leave behind would be Julia's toiletries and one bag with a change. "Just in case," she said. "After all, we're paid up for another day . . . if you need the place . . ." Sam had hung up on Julia's sputters.

Now, riding silently in the elevator with Brad, her thoughts were on a similar ride only the night before. She wondered if Brad was remembering.

Once inside the suite, Julia collected her toilet items from the bathroom, finished packing the bag and checked the rooms for any forgotten items. Satisfied, she closed and locked the door.

Taking her bag and guiding her to the elevators, Brad rode down with her, once again in silence. She did not want to tarry in the suite for the vivid memories of their night together in that bedroom had danced before her like a taunting puppet. Brad had been silent, remaining in the foyer, leaning casually against the door, as if he too did not want to linger.

Samantha's happy greeting was in strong contrast to the somber mood of both Julia and Brad when they entered her apartment. Giving her sister a quizzical look when she walked down the hall to the bedroom with her bag, Samantha led Brad to the living room.

Samantha's hectic lifestyle did not lend to impeccable housekeeping. Using a service was her luxury, but even now she cleared an armchair of various discarded outfits. The apartment decor was helter-skelter. Many items were flea market finds, such as the big faded tuxedo sofa and the art deco blue glass coffee table. The hardwood floors were bare and the walls were stark white, serving as the perfect foil for myriad colorful paintings and posters. Interspersed were blow-ups of Samantha's magazine covers.

"Well. Did Julia like your view of Paris?" Sam asked, her manner inquisitive, hoping Brad would lighten up before Julia joined them.

Brad's eyes flickered. He eyed her silently before saying, "It's hard to say." He looked away, a shadow falling over his face before turning back to her. With unsmiling eyes he said, "Perhaps you'll tell me. After you two have talked."

Hurt, then anger leapt into Sam's eyes. For a moment she was bewildered at his brusque manner towards her, but her eyes softened as she left her perch on the armchair, sitting beside him on the sofa. Touching his shoulder gently, she spoke in a soft voice, "Brad, I'm going to tell you what I told Julia when she first arrived in Paris." Her look was serious. "Regardless of what's happening between you, I want to keep you as my friend." A deep sigh escaped. "OK with you?"

At Samantha's words, he smiled taking her hand. "Little one, you are wiser than all of us." He squeezed her hand. "OK with me."

Giving Brad's shoulder a firm squeeze and excusing herself, she went in search of her sister.

"Ju?"

"Here, Sam. Come in," Julia said as she got up from the bed, smoothing the chenille spread.

"What's wrong?" Sam walked to Julia, putting an arm around her sister's shoulders. She did not miss the sadness in Julia's eyes. "Are you unhappy?"

"No, Sam. Not unhappy."

"Your day with Brad . . . wasn't it good?" Sam persisted.

"Yes," She turned to Sam. "It was good. But, I'm afraid, not good enough." She was silent for a moment before adding, "Even so, we're lunching together tomorrow." A wistful sigh escaped Julia's lips.

"What?" Sam's eyes were full of questions. "Have you changed your mind about staying on a few extra days? You should Julia. You need more than two days to iron this thing out with Brad. Please stay."

Julia looked at her sister and smiled, tweaking her ear.

"No, funny face. I was tempted, but I never changed my reservation. I'll be leaving as planned, day after tomorrow." She looked out of the bedroom window down at the quiet street near the Left Bank Sam lived on. The small café across the street, with a few diners taking in the street scene, revived her pleasant impressions of her visit . . . the people she'd met, running into Brad. With a pang stinging her heart, she said, "I'll be coming back, Sam. I'll be back."

"Does Brad know?"

"That I'm leaving?" She shrugged. "More or less. I told him I was leaving soon. I wasn't specific."

"Somehow I don't think the idea will sit too well with him."

"Really?"

"Just a hunch."

"I think he'll be fine when I'm gone. Just fine," Julia said as she headed towards the living room.

"No, I don't think so . . . and neither will you," Sam muttered to herself as she followed behind her sister to rejoin Brad.

"I don't believe I did that. Why did you let me eat all that?" Julia groaned, rubbing her stomach. "You encouraged me. Two desserts!" she exclaimed. "Sinful."

Chuckling at her discomfort, Brad smiled warmly at Julia. He had enjoyed watching her savor the different dishes he'd suggested. Taillevent, the bistro he had chosen, was a favorite haunt of his, so he knew the selections well. Knowing Julia's passion for chocolate, he couldn't resist tempting her with the delicious confections.

His heart was full of love for her. Longing to pour out his feelings, he held back. Since their visit to the Cathedral, a change had come over her. It appeared that a wave of sorrow had washed over her, leaving a residue of sadness. Several times he had caught her looking at him, her eyes shadowed, but she would quickly cover them with her long lashes. She would start a sentence, then quickly change the subject to whatever scene was before them. She was having great difficulty about something and he wished he knew how to help her. Though he sensed her need to talk, he avoided pressing her for fear of pushing her farther away.

So instead, he reached for her hands, grasping them in his.

"Having fun?" he asked gravely.

Julia felt a warm stirring in her body at his touch. She looked at her hands in his, then twisted them so that she held his hands as well.

Looking intently at him she said, her voice low and soft, "Yes, I am. Thank you. I will always remember this time in Paris."

So that's it. Brad's eyes narrowed, his thoughts racing. She's leaving. Pulling his hands from hers, he sat back in his chair. His eyes never left hers. His voice husky, he asked, "When?"

Startled at the abrupt severing of his touch, Julia flinched at his harsh tone. Is he really sad at my leaving or merely annoyed at losing a playmate so soon?

"At three tomorrow," she replied.

The intake of Brad's breath was audible.

"Why?" he rasped. "You've at least two weeks to go before

starting your new position . . . so it's not that."

He regarded her with veiled eyes. "Or is there some other pressing 'business'. . .?" His questions hung in the air.

The flare up of Julia's anger at his tone and implication quelled almost instantly. Sadly, she realized how his mistrust and misguided thoughts led to their last angry parting in New York. She was determined to clear the air this time. She would leave with his respect, if not his love.

"Brad," she began, "you and I have been dancing all around what's deep inside both of us. We've played our little games, loved one another, enjoyed our excursions, all with some dark specter hovering over us. No, let me finish," she said as Brad started to speak. "And what a ghost," she continued. "After-shave and an electric shaver." Julia's short laugh was humorless. Her dark eyes glinted. "I do not and have never had a live-in lover. Jim Anderson is my co-worker, colleague, friend, escort, and business travel buddy." Her voice growing more distant as she spoke, Julia went on to explain the presence of Jim's toiletries in her bathroom. The early morning shoots, the crazy-hour flights and his mad dashes through airport corridors to make the plane. She stopped speaking.

She gazed at him sadly. "You left with such hatred in your heart for me and I didn't know why." Her eyes closed briefly. "The horrible things you said to me . . ." Her lips quivered, but she bit them and continued. "After you left, I traced your steps. That's when I realized . . ." She struggled to go on, her eyes moist with unshed tears. "You never asked, Brad. You didn't trust me."

"Julia. I didn't–couldn't know. How could I? You're a single beautiful woman, living alone . . ."

"You pre-judged me, Brad. Your mistrust—after all we had shared. You destroyed those beautiful feelings. Why didn't you just ask?"

"Don't you understand that I couldn't? It was all I could do to keep my hands off you. I wanted to shake you. I felt used . . . betrayed."

"After you left, that's what I felt. Betrayed." Julia's tone was sad.

Tense moments of silence passed.

"What made you come to Paris?"

"Sam invited me again. There was a message on my machine when I got back home that afternoon. After you left, I contacted her."

"I left the next day," Brad said.

She raised her eyes to him questioningly.

"That's why I wanted that night to be special." His gaze was somber. "I had planned to tell you while we were out. Unexpected business came up. I had to leave."

Julia did not speak.

He cleared his throat. "When we met here in Paris," he began, "you'd changed. You appeared not to have remembered–or cared about us, what we were." His eyes appeared glazed as if deep in thought. He frowned. "And then, that night . . ." he gasped. "You were so beautiful. But the look in your eyes, the seductive game you were playing. I just played back. You can't deny that you wanted me too," he said harshly.

"No." Her voice was barely a whisper. "No. I can't. I was trying my damnedest to seduce you. You see, Brad, I'd decided to fight back. To fight for you. But . . . I didn't know my enemy and . . . I lost."

His stare was one of puzzlement.

"I didn't know what weapon to use and I lost." A broken sigh escaped her lips. " I thought if I put aside my anger and let you see into my heart, you'd know that I wasn't playing games with you." A shadow fell over her face. "I thought that when you saw this," she softly tapped the opal, "you would begin to understand . . . that . . . I love you. I've loved you since the day I saw you in my mother's kitchen . . ." Her voice ended in a sob that wrenched Brad's insides. Her words hit him like a thunderbolt. He could feel the blood rushing to his head.

"What did you say?" he rasped. "Julia. What are you doing?"

Julia had taken the opal ring off her finger and laid it on the table before Brad.

"I thought that you would see and understand. These few days we've been together, the thoughts and feelings we shared. But yesterday, in St. Severin . . . strange . . . it was then that I realized I'd lost the battle to win your love. Whatever hurt you so that you've closed your heart to me, to anyone who would help you, must have been so traumatic for you." She sighed, her chest lifting slightly. "I can't break through. Whatever it is, you're going to have to work through it. I hope you do, Brad. You deserve more than what you're allowing yourself."

Julia stood up, motioning Brad to stay.

"I'm taking a taxi back to Sam's. Please. Let me do this. I must be alone now, Brad." She reached out and softly ran her fingers against his cheek. "Goodbye, Brad," she whispered. "Be good to yourself."

Brad stood staring after Julia, too dazed to follow her. When he finally roused himself he reached the door of the café to see her enter a taxi that quickly left the curbside, becoming part of the crazy traffic maze. Slowly he returned to the table. Sipping a martini, he sat brooding, staring at the wet rings the glass left on the table as he glided it back and forth.

Chapter XI

"Brad!" Sam's voice was filled with surprise. "Come in," she said, leading him into the living room.

"I have to see Julia before she leaves," Brad said brusquely. I want to go to the airport with you. Is that OK? He looked at Sam questioningly when she remained silent.

"She's gone, Brad."

"When?" His voice was even, controlled.

"The early flight. There was a cancellation."

Brad's eyes appeared to cloud over before he closed them, his hand moving back and forth over his throbbing temples. Then, as if in a daze, he walked to the door. Hesitating, he turned, walking back to where Sam was standing quietly watching him. He bent down and kissed her forehead. "Goodbye, little one." He gave her a quick hug. "I'll be back and forth for the next few months. But remember, call me when you need a friend. Right?" He turned and was gone before Sam could answer.

She stood staring at the closed door, her eyes misting. "You do the same, Brad." she whispered to the silent room.

"Hi, boss," Jim Anderson said when he heard Julia's voice.

"Jim." Her voice was threatening.

"OK, OK, so you're not the boss yet. What's two more weeks?"

"Jim, I'm coming in tomorrow. My vacation's over."

Jim's silence prompted Julia to ask, "Anything wrong, Jim?" She sounded concerned.

"Are you sure you're ready?"

"I'm ready. I met with Joe yesterday. We went over some things. Yes, I'm ready. How about you?"

"You'll do fine, Julia."

"I know. I feel it. Besides, in two weeks Joe will start coming in for a few hours to tie up some loose ends. He insisted." She hesitated, then said, "Jim, would you announce a staff meeting for tomorrow morning at ten?"

Jim chuckled into the receiver. "Atta girl. Plunge right in. For a minute there I thought you had left that old spunk in some Paris café. That's my girl." His voice serious, he said, "Are you really back, Julia?"

"I'm back, Jim. And jumping in with two feet." She hung up the phone and picked up the portfolio Joe had given her. She began to read, her brow furrowed as she pored over the contents.

In the weeks that followed, Julia spent long hours at her office, often returning home exhausted. Although in the past, she had worked closely with Joe as his associate to prepare for the takeover of his duties, manning the helm was a totally different ball game. Pending decisions that would have been Joe's were now unceremoniously hers. Where she and Jim used to work on some assignments, now she felt a slight twinge of jealousy when she saw him with his new associate, their heads together over a problem.

She missed getting out, checking new shooting sites, chattering with the other associates about the mundane aspects of the job. She knew the office staff was proud of her accomplishments, but she felt their shyness and unwillingness to share their lives with her as before. Her "Free Advice" sign had somehow disappeared when she had moved into her new office. She never bothered to have it replaced.

Julia loved her job and would not have traded places with Jim. His new associate partner was young, pretty, ambitious, and Jim often joked that she had better forget about succeeding Julia in the unlikely event of Julia leaving the company. She was not even to *think* about it.

As summer faded into fall, Julia hardly noticed the change of seasons until pumpkin posters and cardboard witches began appearing everywhere.

Where did Labor Day go? she wondered. Since her projects were always projected at least five months ahead, she found it easy to lose track of time. Her head and desk were filled with Valentine images and Easter displays vying for equal time.

Soon the posterboard novelties turned to turkeys, and store windows were dressed in Santas and tinsel.

When the alarm sounded, Julia muttered 'damn' and reached over to press the snooze alarm off. Turning over, she snuggled deeper into the hunter-green paisley bed coverings. It was election day and she had the day off. Her plan was to stay in bed all day; her only activity would be that of calling her parents.

Julia smiled to herself thinking about her mother's last message left on the "box" as her mother called it. "Call or we're coming up. Can you come for Christmas?" That was all.

"Christmas," Julia sighed. "Where did the time go?" She turned her head toward the window. Through the parted green drapes, the early morning sky looked gray and cloud-drenched.

"How unfair that nature would decide the fate of the candidates." She thought rather smugly that she need only take the elevator down to the lobby to vote.

Luxuriating in the warmth of her down comforter, she did not want to stir. Lazily, she tossed the covers back and got up. Donning a robe she padded barefoot on the plush carpet to stand at the window. She stared up at the sky looking for signs of the snow flurries reported in last night's weather forecast. Seeing none, she stared into the distance, a faraway memory crowding her mind. A sweltering day in July. Two people, tenderly and tentatively getting acquainted, laughing hilariously at making plans for the first snowfall. A chill swept over her body.

Pulling the robe closer and slipping into her scuffs, she went to the bathroom to wash and brush her teeth before putting the coffee on.

Replacing the bottle of mouthwash on the shelf suddenly conjured feelings of *déjá vu*: the image of another bottle in that same space flashed before her. She grimaced when she remembered removing the after-shave and the shaving case, tossing them into the trash basket. How two such harmless objects became the catalyst to ruin the relationship between two people was still unfathomable to Julia.

She shook her head in disbelief, vowing not to rehash the painful subject in her mind. When she returned from Paris, she had immersed herself in her work, learning the phases of her new position. Her diligent and efficient performance earned kudos from her boss. He also encouraged her to work more independently, thus giving her the confidence to make major decisions after careful preparation.

Rarely absent from work, she invariably stayed late. Giving it some thought, she realized that today was her first real vacation since Labor Day. Telling herself that her body needed the rest, she turned down a movie date with an old friend.

Julia had been both surprised and flattered at the offer. She knew that she was sadly negligent about keeping in touch and returning calls to her friends. The last date she had was—in Paris.

Her face clouded. Julia had erased the image of Brad from her consciousness. To remember him–their days in New York and in Paris—was extremely painful. She had been proud of the way she had stilled her heart.

But her accomplishment had been short-lived. In September, while watching the late news, Brad's face flashed on the screen. The news story that followed was read excitedly by the news anchor. "Bradford Coleman of TAMA Corporations was exonerated of all charges in the near-fatal illness that befell two customers earlier this year . . ." The television personality then went on to explain the circumstances surrounding the incident. Brad was shown briefly giving an interview. Julia looked intently at Brad as he spoke.

Though the occasion was a joyous one, Brad answered questions in a polite but curt manner. His dark eyes were cold and lifeless, the all too brief smile stiff and humorless. And then the image was gone.

The next day Julia read a full account in *The New York Times.* She was happy that Brad could put the nasty business behind him and get on with his life. A life that would never include her. She quickly chased away those negative thoughts, content in the knowledge that she had a thriving and satisfying career. She had set a goal, reached it and was living her dream.

Taking her coffee into the living room, Julia snuggled under a fleecy blanket on the sofa, settling down to watch the "*Today Show,*" when the telephone rang. Annoyed, she glanced at it, not getting up to answer the ring, letting her machine take the message. There was a long pause after the beep. Thinking the caller decided to hang up, she shrugged but nearly choked on the hot brew when she heard his voice.

"The first snowfall. Will you come? Call me, Julia."

That was all. He hung up, the machine clicking as the message was saved.

"Brad." Her voice was a whisper. She sat for a long while, her drink growing cold while she stared at the TV, unaware of the show.

When Brad left Sam's apartment after being told Julia had gone, he drove with no destination, drove the streets of Paris. Soon he found himself on familiar boulevards and avenues. He drove past the café where he'd first seen Julia–heard her musical laugh. He passed the church, St. Severin, where she had sat in awe of its timeless beauty. He did not stop, refusing to enter for fear of evoking painful memories.

He found he had driven to the Place de la Concorde. Just ahead was the Angelique Hotel. Brad pulled into the driveway and got out, giving the car keys to the valet. Soon he was in the cocktail lounge seated at the same table he had shared with Julia several nights before. He barely tasted the smooth Hennessy sliding down his throat. The bouquet he smelled was the faint scent of lilacs. He closed his eyes and her beautiful image swam in a dizzying arc behind his closed lids. In anguish he twisted the glass in circular motion on the table, staring into the pool of amber liquid.

The words Julia spoke to him reverberated in his mind. "I love you." Those three words. They had sent electric shock waves to his toes. No woman had told him that. Ever. Not since Laura had died. The pain in Julia's voice . . . and he had let her go. Had he been too selfish and self-centered not to have seen through the facade? He knew deep within himself that he had been wrong. The night of their lovemaking, when she allowed him to touch her hair, when she had murmured something about chasing the ghosts away, he knew then. Yet he held back. He'd waited. For what? And now she was gone.

What was it she had said? "You've closed your heart . . ." And he had, never allowing another woman inside, never wanting to be hurt again. Then she had entered his life. Wrongfully, he had accused her of deceit.

Brad finished his drink and ordered another. His immediate thought was to fly to New York to ask her forgiveness. But would she listen? Would she even care after the hurt he caused her? He took a sip of the mellow liquid, letting it slide slowly down his throat. Setting the glass firmly on the table, his hand wrapped around it tightly, his eyes narrowed. A bare nod of his head and he had made a decision. He would let Julia get on with her life–one that did not include him. She was embarking on a new journey and she could do without outside obstacles to obscure her success. She had worked hard to advance her career. She didn't need him in her life. She was a beautiful person inside and out and she would find love again when she was ready.

The thought of Julia in another man's arms burned his gut. "Whoever you are, you'd better be good to her," Brad muttered, envisioning a faceless phantom. Aloud, he whispered, "Goodbye, sweet Julia." Signaling the waiter for the check and leaving a bill on the tiny tray, he left the lounge, his head bowed as he walked out into the early evening.

The valet moved towards him, but Brad motioned him away. He had decided to walk the several blocks to his hotel, thinking to send someone for the car in the morning.

Almost regretting his decision, grimly he walked unwavering along the crowded streets. There were lovers everywhere: in sidewalk cafés, walking arm-in-arm, kissing shamelessly, cuddling on benches. Remembering his own walks and excursions in the hypnotic city, his chest grew heavy. He stopped and stared at one couple so intently that they became nervous and hurried away, giving him puzzled backward glances.

A humorless smile cracking his mouth, Brad continued walking. Her image floating before him, he whispered again, "Goodbye, sweet Julia."

The late July sun the next day was hot and the streets were crowded with tourists and office workers seeking a cool lunchtime refuge.

Brad had finished his meal in the fast food establishment and was tasting the popular syrupy crushed ice drink flavored with cherries. Not bad, he thought, taking another swallow, the ice soothing his parched throat. He sat back and observed the operation as he had been doing since he walked in over half an hour ago. The business was similar to his own and was his main competitor. Noting nothing out of the ordinary, his brow furrowed. His friendly interrogation of the staff produced no knowledge of David Jensen. After awhile, he sighed deeply. It was time to make a call to William Brooks. Time to notify the executive offices of Puffin's Restaurants the findings of Brad's hunch and JJ's research.

Days later Brad received a telegram from William Brooks. "Congratulations," it read. "Your suspicions are on the money. David Jensen on our advice is being investigated by his executive offices. They informed us our suspicions warranted a thorough investigation of their executive employees." The messagegram went on to explain that William would place a call to Brad the next day with a full explanation of the details.

* * *

When the call came through, Brad listened without interruption. Finally, he said, his mouth a grim line, "Thanks William. You'll handle it with the media?" Nodding his head to William's reply and after giving him some instructions, Brad hung up the phone. He lay full length on the couch, eyes closed, recalling William's report. Running his hand repeatedly across his forehead, he appeared to be rubbing away bitter memories. Curiously he thought about David Jensen. What must a man be driven to in order to take such measures? To flirt with death–not his, but that of innocent people.

According to JJ's sleuthing and later Puffin's Corporation findings, David Jensen, a fifty-six-year-old executive, was about to be lost in the shuffle as a result of his company's reorganization. Fearing the end of his career with Puffin's and the uncertainty of success elsewhere, he took a desperate gamble. Preying on the TAMA Corporation scandal of a few years ago, he devised his vicious plan to bring unfavorable publicity to the business giant.

His aim was to devastate TAMA's newly-opened restaurant in Paris.

The carefully-orchestrated poisonings of the customers by Jensen and his inside accomplice worked; the Paris business was seriously affected due to the adverse publicity. In turn, Puffin's Restaurant flourished under the guidance of Jensen, who had maneuvered into the position of Paris operations manager. With his success in the foreign market, he was no longer affected by the corporation's reorganization plans.

The complete report of allegations, including dates, the name of Jensen's accomplice and positive proof of being seen in the Bronx store with his helper, was sent to the executive offices of the Puffin's chain.

Weeks later, in early September after his company's thorough investigation of the allegations, David Jensen was arrested. The two corporation heads jointly held a news conference. Brad and TAMA were completely exonerated of any wrong-doing and public apologies were made. Furthermore, the victims were to be compensated for medical bills and pain and suffering.

The days and weeks following the story found Brad restless in Paris. With the advent of fall and his renewed popularity, he was the most sought-after bachelor in the city. At one posh party he met Henry Montgomery, who inquired about Julia. The mention of her name caused Brad's eyes to cloud. He tersely responded that he was "in the dark" and walked away while the other man stared at him in puzzlement.

He saw Samantha at least three times, but each time she was on the run, busy fulfilling her contracts, packing and sending furnishings and clothing back to the States in preparation for leaving

Paris in December to start her new life.

As the end of October neared, Brad, tiring of the round of parties and with the operation running smoothly, abruptly decided to end his stay. He made arrangements to leave Paris as soon as possible. A week later he was home in New York.

Brad had been home for a week before he called Helen. For months in Paris he'd worked incessantly, kept all social commitments, never leaving himself free time. He had found that his idle mind would conjure the image of a beautiful face with dancing eyes and delightful smile. He also imagined the twinkle of a musical laugh. To dispel the mood-altering images, he worked or socialized, escorting his incessantly prattling female companions to the many Paris bashes.

In New York, his driven schedule continued, but this time, work was his only outlet. Feeling guilty about his lack of concern for Helen, he finally called her from his office. Surprised to hear from him, she was very pleased and would not accept no for an answer to dinner at her home that evening. He accepted, hanging up feeling good about making the overdue call.

Helen gasped when she saw Brad. He gave her a bear hug and tears sprang to her eyes when she felt his thin cheek graze hers. When he removed his overcoat, her breath intake was audible. Though he was dressed well, navy blue suit, pale blue shirt and red paisley tie, the amount of space between his neck and shirt collar was clearly visible. His face was gaunt and his eyes looked haunted. Helen was reminded of the way Brad looked years before when he had lost his family. No, she thought. Not again.

In the kitchen where she had dinner prepared, he helped her set the table, talking non-stop about his doings in Paris, the business, the past media coverage. He stopped to thank her for the messagegram she'd sent to him, telling him to put the mess behind him. As they ate, Helen talked of her jewelry shows and fairs. She never mentioned the opal ring. She remembered when he had picked it up his eyes had sparkled and his step was light. Now, he looked as if his heart weighed heavy.

"Brad," she said as they carried coffee cups into the comfortable living room, "how have you really been?"

Brad looked at Helen a long moment before answering. Wearily he closed his eyes. Helen could always read him. She could interpret what was left unsaid. She never interfered, except when she thought it was extremely necessary. Apparently she thought it was time. He looked at her. "Surviving," he said softly.

"Just barely." Her voice was stern. "How is Julia? Did she like the ring?" she continued, daring to mention the gemstone.

His eyes flickered. "She loved it." He paused. "She gave it back to me. I've not seen or heard from her in months."

Both were silent until Helen spoke. "Tell me about it."

Brad shrugged, his eyes filling with pain as he recalled the last time he had seen Julia. "I messed up. I was an idiot. She offered her love to me and I rejected it–and her."

Helen remained silent.

When Brad spoke again his voice sounded lifeless. He began relating the events over the past few months, from the time he picked up the ring from Helen until he returned to New York.

When he finished he got up and went to the kitchen, returning with fresh cups of coffee. "She's started a new career, a new life. I'm sure she's happy now."

"You know you don't believe that."

"That's what I want to believe."

"Men," Helen spat out. "So you are not going to pick that phone up to call her?"

"Why interfere after all these months?" He wearily ran a hand through his hair. "Maybe in the beginning she would have listened, but now . . ." His hands spread hopelessly.

"She's probably involved anyway." He closed his eyes at the thought.

When Helen did not speak, he raised his eyes to look at her.

"No comment?" he said wryly.

"One," Helen replied. "Call her."

Brad raised a brow. "That's it?"

"That's it."

Brad got up, jammed his hands in his pocket and began pacing the room. Turning to Helen he said, "Suppose she's. . ."

"Suppose what? Have you gotten to where you are with a lifetime of supposes? I think not." Helen crossed her arms and glared at Brad. "Where's your head, man? Why do you think that young woman ran off to Paris in such a hurry–after cutting her Virginia vacation short to follow you to New York?"

"But . . ."

"But nothing. She wanted to put as much distance as she could between you and the horrible thoughts you had of her." She paused to take a breath. "Why, when she first saw you in that café in Paris, it's a wonder she didn't cut you dead." Helen eyed him intently. "*That* was a woman in love. And the ring? She was actually wearing it? That *definitely* should have penetrated."

"I didn't know," Brad's voice was low. He looked at Helen helplessly. He walked back to the sofa, sitting down heavily. "Not at first. Not until the last day. But by then it was too late."

Helen's eyes softened when she heard the misery in his voice. "Men," she repeated, this time softly. "Brad," she said, "it's not too late. Call her."

"How would you know?"

With a twinkle of her eye and an exaggerated shrug of her shoulders Helen replied, "Am I ever wrong?" Then smiling, "Call her."

Brad said goodnight to Helen hours later and driving home he thought about her response. He chuckled. Response? he asked himself. Then he grinned, wiping imaginary sweat from his brow. "Whew!" he said.

Once inside his apartment, Brad continued to dwell on his talk with Helen and his admission of his relationship with Julia. He walked about the apartment. He stood at the entrance to his bedroom, leaning against the door, gazing at his bed. He could almost smell Julia's scent, feel her hot breath on his neck, his chest. His stomach churned. Turning away, he went back to the living room. He pulled the drapes back from the terrace window and stared out. The lights from the passing cars twinkled like so many red and white Christmas balls.

A painful memory flittered across his mind. A summer day when two people pledged to meet at the same spot at the first snowfall of the year. Snow. Flurries were predicted for tomorrow, he thought. "No significant accumulation," the weather-man had said.

"But," mused Brad, "are they ever wrong?" He laughed harshly.

Then, a frown wrinkled his brow. Would she remember? Would she come? Why should she? he questioned himself furiously.

Helen's words invaded his thoughts. "Call her."

Still staring at the multicolored flashing balls of light, Brad muttered, "I will."

Chapter XII

Weeks had passed since Brad's voice sounded over her message machine. Julia never responded. She had spent the rest of that day busying herself with catch-up chores in the apartment and casting her vote in the lobby where the voting machines had been set up for that precinct. She jumped when the phone rang again, only to find it was her mother. For days after Brad's call, she'd come home expecting to find another message, but there were no more. She began to relax. Thoughts of him disappeared as she immersed herself in her work. At times, she wished she could reach behind her and massage the ache between her shoulder blades. The round of holiday parties had begun, some social, but most business. Sometimes she went with Jim, other times she went unescorted. She left them nearly always feeling sad, especially when she looked at the couples who were obviously in love.

Though the weather was bitterly cold, there had been no snowfall. The flurries predicted a few weeks back never happened. Once, flurries of no consequence appeared briefly for about ten minutes.

The Friday after Thanksgiving dawned gray and gloomy. The

bus ride to work was quiet and there was less traffic. She was grateful to reach her warm office, for it was blustery cold outside. She looked around at the sparsely staffed office, realizing that most of the workers had taken the day off. There was very little activity. She could have taken the day too, but didn't, not wanting to develop a case of the holiday blues. She had Thanksgiving dinner with her next-door neighbors, joining them at their insistence. They had heard her going and coming when she did her laundry and had invited her over. She hadn't stayed long, but thanking them, left soon after they'd eaten.

Julia smiled when she thought about the sisters and their generosity. When she left she had carried a large bag filled with foil-wrapped packets of delicious food: turkey, stuffing, butternut squash, mince and sweet potato pie, collard greens. "So you won't have to eat out tomorrow," they said. She was thankful now that she'd accepted their care package, because she neither felt like eating out nor preparing her own dinner.

Her buzzer sounded. Julia looked at her calendar, puzzled. There were no appointments scheduled. When she inquired who it was and the purpose for the visit, the receptionist replied that it was a "Helen Stevenson." The business was personal, she said.

Personal? I don't know how personal this business could be, thought Julia, especially if I don't even know a Helen Stevenson. "Send her in," Julia told the receptionist.

A moment later, through the glass walls Julia saw the outer door open to admit a woman. As she walked purposely toward Julia, she smiled. What arresting features, thought Julia. She's a handsome woman.

Julia rose from her desk, walking to the door to greet her visitor. Try as she might, Julia could not place her among faces she had ever seen before.

"Thank you for seeing me, Ms. Hart. My name is Helen Stevenson." Julia motioned to her guest to sit on the black leather couch. Julia pulled up a matching armchair and sat, curious about the striking woman and the reason for her visit.

"Would you care to remove your coat?" Julia asked.

"No, that won't be necessary. I'm not staying that long."

The well-modulated tones and friendliness of her eyes piqued

Julia's curiosity further. "How may I help you, Ms. Stevenson?" The woman smiled back in reply, causing further heightening of Julia's curiosity. Why should a complete stranger appear to be so friendly? Had they met before?

"I'm Bradford Coleman's former mother-in-law, Ms. Hart."

There was a long moment of silence.

"I'm here to ask your help," Helen continued, her eyes warily watching Julia's reaction to her words.

Julia stiffened at the mention of Brad's name, visibly taken aback when the woman revealed her identity, the statement hitting Julia like a sledgehammer. She emitted a tiny gasp.

With great difficulty, Julia said, "Mother-in-law?"

"Former. My daughter, Brad's wife, is dead, Ms. Hart. Brad's been a widower for almost eight years, now."

The woman's voice became quieter when she mentioned her daughter, her eyes saddening as she continued to look steadily at Julia.

Julia's heart thumped wildly against her chest. Her mind raced back to snatches of conversation she'd heard about Brad during the time of the first scandalous food poisonings. She vaguely remembered how the news media reports had always referred to him as the "elusive bachelor." Brad had never spoken of his wife. Once when she and Brad had gotten into a discussion about past relationships, he'd sternly told her, "I'm no longer married," a shadow falling over his darkened face. Julia had been satisfied that there was no abused, neglected wife waiting somewhere for her man to return. Since then, there was never any further discussion about either of their past relationships. They had been engrossed only in one another.

But Brad, a widower for eight years. How sad. He must have loved her dearly, finding it too painful to speak of her death. Now, she looked at the woman with the lovely silver hair. She can't be too old, Julia thought. What a face of character she has, she marveled. And her jewelry. Such pieces. Julia was certain that the rings and the earrings were one-of-a-kind. Helen Stevenson piqued her interest.

She said, her voice soft, "I'm sorry. I didn't know. Brad never mentioned . . ." her voice trailed away.

"He never does." Helen paused, her brow wrinkled. "That was a bad time for him."

"Ms. Stevenson, you said you need my help. I don't understand . . ."

"Helen. Please call me Helen. And may I call you Julia? I have been all along," Helen added with a wry smile.

"Of course, please do." Julia's look was one of total perplexity.

Helen stirred. Shrugging out of her ivory camel hair coat, she said, "This is taking longer than I anticipated." In the same movement she opened her black leather purse and removed an envelope. Lifting the flap, she took out some snapshots, handing one to Julia.

Julia reached for it. The young woman staring back at her with the perfect oval face was a stunning beauty. Julia raised her questioning eyes to Helen's.

"My daughter, Laura."

"She's gorgeous. Just beautiful," murmured Julia.

"As you are," Helen said sadly.

"I beg your pardon . . ." What a strange thing to say, thought Julia.

"You are a beautiful woman, Julia. Just like my daughter Laura was." Before Julia spoke, Helen handed her two more pictures. "My grandson, Omar, my granddaughter, Tasha. They are dead, too."

Julia looked at the tiny laughing faces. She need not ask if they were Brad's children: although Omar had a resemblance, Tasha was the very image of him. Tears misted Julia's lashes. She was remembering the time in Virginia when Brad had responded so warmly to the youngsters who in turn spontaneously gravitated toward him. She stared at the pictures. Dead. She shook her head sadly. So young, she thought. Handing the pictures back to Helen, she remained silent, waiting for her to explain.

"Laura, Tasha and Omar died in a car crash. Laura was driving. She and Omar died instantly. Tasha lived in a coma for nine days. She never regained consciousness." Helen's voice was almost devoid of emotion as she forced herself to continue her story.

Julia's heart ached for Helen—for Brad. Oh, Brad, she whispered silently. My love . . .

"Brad was a madman for weeks after. I saw an average, fun-loving young man turn into a cold, hard, calculating, driven machine." Helen paused, as if remembering brought pain to her heart. She looked hard at Julia.

"He's like that again . . . only worse. He's heading for serious health problems if he doesn't pull himself up short," she said, her voice growing stern. She didn't allow Julia to speak, but went on, starting from the time before the accident. She told Julia about the argument between Laura and Brad, Laura's spoiled and selfish ways, her jealousy over Brad's dedication to his business. She told of Laura's constant craving for attention. "Men saw it and were willing to oblige her. She loved to be the object of adoration at parties. Brad saw what was happening and hated it. They argued about her behavior. She never tired of the socializing, refusing to listen to her husband's objections." Helen stopped, her eyes closed briefly.

"Please, you don't . . ." Julia began.

"No, dear, you must know." Her voice was strained. "The night of the accident, they'd argued. She was bringing the children to me to babysit. She'd decided to attend a party without Brad." Her breathing was heavy. "The roads were slick from the driving rain. The curve was taken too fast. She lost control." The silence became heavy in the room after Helen finished speaking. Only an occasional ring of the phone in the outer offices and distant voices marred the quiet.

Finally, Julia spoke. "Ms. Steven . . . Helen . . . I'm so sorry."

After a long moment, Helen said, her voice weary, "Years after the death of his family, Brad found himself to be a successful man. His dogged determination netted him the goals he'd set for himself when he and Laura first married. He appeared always to be proving himself." Helen cleared her throat. "Then one day he woke up and realized that he didn't have to prove to himself—to Laura—that he was a hardworking achiever, excellent provider. He was a success."

Helen's eyes softened, her lips widened in a smile. "He began to relax. He vacationed, dated." She stopped, eyeing Julia closely. "He was living as normal a life as he could. I guess you could say he was finally at peace with himself. But, then this summer . . . he changed."

"This summer," Julia echoed.

"I last saw him in July just before he left for Paris on business," Helen said. "He was happy then."

Silence.

"And now?" prompted Julia.

Helen's eyes were sad as she looked into Julia's. "He arrived back in New York at the end of October. He came to see me." A cloud shadowed Helen's face as she remembered. "He looked the same as he had the year he lost his family," she said, her voice husky.

Julia looked down at her clasped hands. Her heart ached for the pain the other woman must be feeling. She loves Brad very much, she thought. Oh, Brad, she whispered silently, what's wrong? What are you doing to yourself?

Aloud she said, her voice low and controlled, "He's ill." Her voice was factual.

"Not yet. He's lost weight. He . . . has that lost look about him again. His eyes are cold, lifeless," Helen's voice became distant.

Both woman were silent, each with their minds on Brad.

Helen spoke first. She noticed that Julia's hands were ringless except for the tiny opal on her left pinky finger.

She said, "Just before Brad left for Paris, he picked up an opal ring that I'd designed for him." She paused before looking pointedly at Julia's finger, then curiously stared into her eyes. "It was for you."

Julia gasped. "You made . . . it's so beautiful. So unique." Her eyes filled with admiration for Helen. Now she understood the look of exclusivity of Helen's silver jewelry.

Helen nodded her head in acknowledgement of the compliment, but said nothing.

Sighing, Julia said, "I don't have it. I gave it back to Brad."

"Yes. I know." Helen quickly continued when she saw the indignant look spring into Julia's eyes. "When Brad returned from your family reunion in July, he was the happiest I'd seen him in years," Helen explained. "He was different. I knew right away that something good was happening in his life. You were that something."

Julia stirred. Her thoughts had flitted back to that tumultuous summer weekend in Virginia. She looked at Helen. Her voice softly curious, she asked, "Why did you show me your daughter's picture, Helen? What is it you want of me? Brad and I are . . . not together. We never were, actually. So I don't understand," she stopped, spreading her hands in a helpless gesture.

"Beautiful women. Don't you see? Brad can't stand the thought of falling in love with another beautiful woman. And he's fallen in love with you." She paused, "He's in love with you and it's killing him."

"Brad's never told me that he loved me."

"Does he have to? You're not one of those empty-headed women who'll punish a man for that. No. I refuse to entertain the thought," Helen said, shaking her head emphatically. "Julia, I'm not here to pry. You must make up your own mind. You both must. But I guess as an older outsider who can see what's happening, I'm breaking the rule, just once." She stood up and began to shrug into her coat. Pausing, one arm in the sleeve, she said, "He hasn't tried to call you or see you since his return?" Her voice was questioning as she stared hard at Julia.

"He called," Julia answered. Fleeting images flashed before her of that cold day several weeks before, her annoyance at the jarring jangle of the telephone bell, her shock at hearing Brad's voice. Aware of Helen's penetrating glance, she repeated, "He did call."

She looked at Helen, her eyes full of misery. "I never returned his call." She saw the look in the older woman's eyes and it pained her. "I loved him. I loved him and he . . . mistrusted me. I knew there was some deep pain . . . I tried to help. . . but . . . I couldn't."

Julia's brow furrowed as she remembered those last moments in Paris.

"I tried," she whispered.

"You still love him." It was a statement.

Julia closed her eyes tightly. When she opened them to look at Helen through misted lashes, she whispered, "Yes."

Helen smiled. Pulling her coat close, tying the sash, she slid her gloves on. For the first time since she walked into the office, her eyes smiled.

"Then call him."

"I can't do that," she whispered. "I've already tried to reach him, and failed. He . . . has to come to terms with himself."

"How do you know he hasn't?" Helen looked at her intently. When Julia appeared puzzled, she said to her gently, "You never returned his call."

"Thanks, William. Yeah, sure. I will. Ummm . . . I promise we'll have that lunch soon. Right after Christmas. Yes, William. I know it's next week. Sure. I'll call. Bye."

Brad sat staring at the phone after he hung up. His thoughts were on William. His friend had called him several times in the past week, both at home, and, as now, at his office. He recognized his friend's concern.

They had had little or no contact since his return from Paris. The one time they did meet at a business meeting, he could see the flicker of worry in his friend's eyes. William, Brad smiled, with his uncanny ability to read him, had asked Brad, "You're still with us, man?" They both knew the reference was to Brad's dropping out when he had lost his family. Brad had replied, "I'm here, man. Still here."

Brad swiveled his chair around until he faced the wide picture window. The gray vertical blinds were opened, allowing him to peer up at an equally gray December sky, the clouds hanging low. Standing up, he stared out of his twelfth-floor window, which overlooked Broadway. The wind whipped about, causing the scurrying shoppers to move quickly in and out of the crowded stores, everyone trying to find that last minute Christmas gift. He scowled, eyes growing dark, and thought about his own holiday shopping. He'd done it all in one day, in one store—Fortunoff's. His two major purchases were for Helen and William, the two people he considered to be his only family. He'd left the rest of the shopping for his employees to his secretary; it also included his Paris staff.

Brad made it a point to stay out of the stores as Christmas neared. Those first few years after the deaths of Omar and Tasha, the look of excitement he saw on the faces of kids caused his heart to wrench with pain. Once he had stopped and listened to the dialogue between a young girl and Santa Claus. He had to leave when the little girl had wistfully asked for another Mommy because hers was now an angel. The sorrow on the face of the man standing with the little girl was too much for Brad to bear.

Since then, he had discreetly directed his staff through his assistant to play Santa at two children's homes every year.

Pushing himself away from the window, he turned to leave the deserted office. His staff had left an hour ago at five o'clock. The darkening sky was threatening to bring the icy rains the stations had been predicting for most of the day. Turning off the lights and locking the office door, Brad headed for the elevator, hating the thought of entering his apartment alone on such a gloomy night. He shuddered and decided to have dinner out, hoping to catch the holiday spirit of the Christmas shoppers and enjoy the good food and glowing warmth of the Veronica Cafe, only a few blocks away on West 51st Street. He knew after a meal in his favorite haunt, his mood would change.

The family restaurant with its friendly staff, burnished stained walnut walls with copper utensils jutting from a wall of exposed brick, lent a cozy atmosphere to the surroundings. Brad knew that he'd enjoy the rich, crisp duck *á l'orange* in peaceful solitude. As he hurried to the restaurant, he knew another reason he feared being alone was that he knew that Julia's voice would not be among his phone messages. For days after he'd called her that morning in November, he'd listen expectantly to his message machine, waiting to hear her soft voice. In the days that followed, his mood grew dark and bitter when it became apparent that she wasn't going to call. He ignored the gnawing pain in his stomach whenever his thoughts turned to her. He'd see the sweet face with the smiling dark eyes and impish grin, sometimes thinking he smelled the sweet scent of violets or lilacs, the perfume she'd worn in Paris.

His steps quickened as he was buffeted by the driving rain. Head lowered, he rushed for the warmth of the restaurant, reaching the door at the same time as a laughing shivering couple. Since Brad already had his hand on the knob, he held the door, allowing the woman to enter and nodded at her companion to follow. He said to Brad, stepping inside, "Thanks, man. Some storm kicking up out here."

Brad nodded in agreement as he shook his coat off, glancing at the couple who stood just in front of him. Something about the man seemed vaguely familiar to him, but Brad couldn't place the voice. The man turned to speak to Brad and suddenly stopped. Recognition leapt into his eyes. "Coleman?" he queried.

Brad remembered. "Anderson. Jim Anderson, right?"

"Yes. We met this summer. Julia . . ."

"I remember," Brad cut him off. Peering closely at the woman, he saw she was not Julia. Feeling oddly relieved, he looked at Jim, his voice lighter, "I . . . Merry Christmas." Brad was a little embarrassed. If Jim was not seeing Julia, then . . . but how could he ask in front of his date? Just then the waitress returned after seating other patrons and said to Jim, "Two? Follow me please."

Brad felt deflated. Seeing the sag of Brad's shoulders, Jim said, "Get seated, Coleman, I'll find you."

A few minutes after Brad sat down, he saw Jim walking toward him. Brad stood up, extending his hand.

After shaking hands, Jim joined him at the table. "Can't stay long. My lady's waiting," he said, looking over to where his companion was seated. Brad followed his gaze. Jim's eyes rested on the young woman who shyly gave him a smile as their eyes met. Her shoulder-length jet black hair framed her dark beige square face. Her light brown eyes flashed a smile at Jim. Brad looked away, instantly feeling melancholy.

He felt Jim's stare. He looked up, saying, "She's very pretty."

Jim said, "Yeah. I think so," as he threw a quick smile at his friend. Turning back to Brad, he said, "She's doing a fine job. But she's not superwoman."

"What?"

"You know who I mean."

Brad's eyes narrowed, but he said nothing.

"Julia took over her new duties with gusto. She's passed the test, but she's not stopping. She's driving herself as if . . . as if she slows down, she's going to have to occupy her thoughts with things other than the job." Jim reached into his breast pocket, pulling out a small beige card. Taking his pen, he wrote something on it, then handed the card to Brad. "That's Julia's private line. You can call her direct." He stood up. "Look, man, I don't know what happened this summer between you two, but from the looks of you both . . . neither of you is going to end this year asa representative of good health ads."

Then, holding out his hand, he said softly, "Call her, man."

Brad stood up, taking Jim's hand, nodding as he stared intently at him. His eyes reflected glimmers of light as he thoughtfully watched Jim walk quickly back to his waiting companion.

His meal unfinished, Brad summoned the waiter for the check. Once leaving the warm interior of the restaurant, the blast of cold air hit him with fury, sending shivers through him. Suddenly he decided walking to the subway and waiting for a cold train seemed less than appealing. Ten minutes later he was huddled in the back of a taxi slowly making its way crosstown to the FDR Drive, then over to the Brooklyn Bridge. His somber mood was caught by the cab driver who tried to engage Brad in conversation but soon gave up, preferring to serenade himself in song.

After Jim had left the table, Brad was visibly shaken by his words. Did he look that bad? he asked himself. So Helen was not exaggerating, he mused, rubbing his temples wearily. His stomach churned when he recalled Jim's words, "She's driving herself . . ." The thought of Julia ill, not having someone to help her. He remembered the story she told him of how her neighbors nursed her through the flu—sick—all alone. His breath came in a rush, the idea of her alone, needing someone, was almost too much for him to bear. The sudden urge washed over him to see her—if only to assure himself that she was well. The refrain, "driving herself," played over and over again in his mind as he paid the driver and exited the cab, hurrying into his apartment building.

Once inside his apartment, he walked immediately to the phone, pressed the message button, removed his coat and waited. He stared intensely at the machine as if it were to blame for not filling his ears with the sound of Julia's voice. Turning away from Helen's voice reminding him about Christmas dinner, he started dejectedly for the bedroom, the machine clicking on another call.

He stopped short, catching his breath, as he heard the voice. "Hello, Brad. It's Julia. I . . . I'm calling to say . . . well, I guess I already said it." She laughed. He could hear the shy nervousness. His chest rose and fell sharply as he listened. "I . . . I'm going out of town on business, Brad. Just want to say, enjoy the holidays. Merry Christmas, Brad."

Away? Going away? No, he thought in anguish. When? Had she left already? Glancing at his watch, noting the hour was nearly eleven, he was torn—he did not want to waken her—but he had to know.

Brad dropped heavily on the couch, a groan escaping his lips. I can't wait 'til morning, he thought. I've got to try. Reaching for the phone, Brad firmly dialed Julia's number. He had never forgotten it. The beat of his heart kept pace with the rise and fall of his chest. Please be there went through his mind as the phone rang and rang.

"Hello?"

His silent plea was answered.

Oh, God. Thank God. He spoke into the receiver, "Julia." He cleared his throat. "Did I wake you? I thought when you didn't answer . . ."

The heavy timbre of his voice sent warm waves rippling up and down her body. The old familiar sensation evoked such pleasant memories that the flush reached the roots of her hair. Seconds of silence passed slowly.

"Are you all right?"

"I'm here, Brad. I was in the shower. I heard the phone when I turned the water off," she said breathlessly. "Would you hold a second?"

"Of course."

Julia wrapped the terry towel around her wet curls and pulled the sash closely around her slender waist, securing the floor-length pale blue terry robe.

"Hi," she said. "I'm decent."

Brad envisioned her nakedness under her robe and the image drove him mad. His voice tight, he asked, "When are you leaving? Can we . . . meet before you leave?" His voice was filled with trepidation. His heart sank at her next words.

"My plane leaves at ten a.m., Brad."

"Oh." For the first time in his life Brad seemed at a loss for words. Moments before, he was like a madman when he thought she'd already gone, and now his tongue felt like peanut butter was glued to the roof of his mouth. "I thought we could meet. But I guess that's out. No chance of a later flight?" he asked hopefully.

"Company business, Brad. I must go."

Scowling into the phone, Brad said, "Can I drive you to the airport?"

"The company car has been scheduled for me."

"Dammit, cancel it, Julia. I want to see you." Then realizing his gaffe, Brad apologized. "I'm sorry. But I must see you before you leave."

Julia closed her eyes tightly. Oh, Brad, she cried silently. I've waited so long to hear your voice, to see you, touch you. For months Julia thought she'd rid her system of Brad; she tried not to think of him, working hard, coming home exhausted. Then came the visit from Helen. Now she knew that Brad lay just beneath her consciousness, always there—where she realized he always would be. When she called and he did not answer, she had felt such a sense of desolation. She told herself that when she returned from her business trip, she would try to reach him again. But now, his demanding voice was on the other end of the line trying so hard to mask his fears and pain. Her heart ached for him–for them.

She answered, "I'll be back day after tomorrow, Brad. It's only a one-day meeting in Baltimore. Can we meet when I return?"

Her voice was soft in his ear. The smoothness of it had the desired effect Julia had intended, for Brad answered in a lower voice, "I guess I'll have to wait," his tone husky. There was a pause. "Will you call when you return?"

"I'll call you, Brad. We'll do lunch."

He caught the smile in her voice. Both were reluctant to hang up, thinking their own private thoughts.

His growl of a laugh sounded in her ear. "Not much snow this year."

"Hardly any at all."

"Julia?"

"Yes?"

"Will you come?"

She was silent. A kaleidoscope of color flashed before her eyes as she remembered the view from his terrace and the words they'd spoken. She feared his rejection. "I . . . I'm not sure, Brad," she finally answered.

Though his heart thumped wildly, he would not press her; he had no right. She would have to come because she wanted to, not because he was holding her to some silly promise made months ago. But when he responded, his voice held all the bottled up fears and pain he'd carried for months, thinking he'd never see her or hear her voice again. He said, his voice low, "I want you to–very much."

He hung up, the sound of the receiver settling on the cradle with such a click of finality caused his heart to pound. The rhythmic beat seemed to resound in the still room.

"Thanks, Harry, I'm on my way down," Julia informed the doorman when he buzzed her on the intercom. Once down in the lobby and out the main entrance, Julia frowned at not spying the familiar dark grey New Yorker her company used. Instead, the distinctive, long, navy blue Lincoln Town Car limousine was parked in front of the building. Just as recognition leapt into her eyes, Brad emerged from the back seat of the limousine. Julia gasped, her heart thudding wildly as she watched Brad walk towards her. His black eyes bored into hers, never wavering. When he reached her, he stopped, staring at her, devouring her hungrily with a smoldering look. After a long moment, he said, his voice husky, "I had to see you." Julia remained motionless, too stunned to speak. Brad took her overnight bag from her hand, lightly touched her elbow, guiding her to the waiting limo.

Finding her voice, she said, "My car . . ."

"I took care of it. Your driver understands you'll make your plane on time," he said brusquely.

As they reached the Lincoln, Roy, Brad's now familiar driver, opened the door for them, smiling and touching his cap to Julia as he helped them inside, putting her bag in the trunk. Roy started the long drive to La Guardia Airport, moving the long vehicle expertly through the heavy traffic on Amsterdam Avenue.

Brad had closed the privacy panel when he entered the limo, and turning to Julia, he spoke quietly. "I've missed you." His voice was hoarse. He reached over, took her hands and removed her soft ivory leather gloves. He held both of her hands tightly in his.

His touch sent millions of excruciating, delicious tingles of fire along her spine. His gaze held hers. Suddenly, leaning over, cupping her chin in his hand, he kissed her. Feeling the touch of her cool lips on his, he groaned, the ache in his chest becoming unbearable. "Sweet Julia," he murmured, his mouth never leaving hers.

A soft cry escaping her bruised lips, Julia reached up and put her arms around Brad's neck, crushing her lips to his. The remembered warmth surged through her body like an opened floodgate. Brad released her lips, kissed her cheek, her neck, and recaptured her mouth.

Finally, her head resting on his chest, her eyelashes moist, she sat quietly, Brad's arms wrapped around her. She tilted her head, looking up at him. "You look awful." Her voice was teasing but sad. She held back a sob.

Brad's face was gaunt and his black eyes appeared lifeless. When she'd seen him walking towards her, her heart went out to him. He looked tired and drawn.

He said, still holding her tightly, "But I feel like I'm sitting on top of the world right now." He gave her a peck on the forehead.

As they drove through the voluminous traffic on Grand Central Parkway, nearing the airport, Julia sat up, straightening her fireman's red coat and fluffing her mussed curls.

"No need. You're as beautiful as ever." His eyes gleamed as he stared at her.

"Brad . . ."

"Julia . . ."

They both laughed as they spoke in unison.

Brad said, "You first."

She smiled sadly at him. Turning away, staring out of the window, she said, "I've thought about what you asked me last night." Her voice was soft as she continued. "I'm not sure that I can . . . that I want to see you again, Brad . . ." Her voice faltered. She went on, turning to face him. "I'm not that strong. I feel that I will have to spend every day that we're together convincing you that I am not Laura."

She felt Brad stiffen, saw his eyes grow cold and distant, before he turned his face from her. Reaching up, she gently turned, him back to her, holding his gaze. She said softly, "Helen came to see me."

Understanding and pain flickered in Brad's eyes but he said nothing, watching her with hooded lids.

Julia continued, holding Brad's hand softly in hers. "I'm sorry for Omar and Tasha–and Laura," she began. "Your pain must have been so great." She swallowed as her throat tightened. She felt the pressure of his hand as he gripped hers. "I've loved you for so long, Brad . . ." He made a sound, as if to speak, but Julia said, "No . . . let me finish." His eyes had a faraway look. "I think I fell in love with you when Sam sent a picture to me. I picked you out of the group. For a year, I tried to figure out what lay behind those sad dark eyes." She smiled at him as he caressed her cheek with his fingers. "Then," she continued, "when I met you in Virginia, I no longer had any doubts. I knew. I fought it at first, but I knew."

Brad whispered her name.

Julia said softly, "In Paris, I didn't know what I was fighting. Now that I know . . ." she stopped, shrugged and spread her hands helplessly.

"Now that you know," he said, "can't you understand what I was feeling about you? How I felt when I saw the cologne, the shaver . . ." His voice was harsh. "I was seeing Laura all over again."

"That's just it," Julia said, her shoulders sagging as she emitted a sigh. "You've seen her in all the beautiful women you've known. You'll continue to see her until you've forgiven her . . . and yourself, and learn to trust again, to trust me."

The limousine was pulling up the ramp to the departing flights. Brad reached out, stopping Julia as she prepared to exit when the car stopped.

"I need you—want you with me—beside me, Julia. You're not saying goodbye. I won't let you. Not again," he growled in a low voice.

"Brad, for now, I must. I need time. Time to think about us. We've hurt one another. I'm just not ready for another rejection. I couldn't handle your suspicions again . . . I couldn't."

"There wouldn't be any." His voice was nearly a bark.

"How can you be so sure?" she replied, her tone easy and controlled. She paused. "Tonight, after the business is finished–will I be alone? Engaged in a wrap-up session with a colleague in the cocktail lounge?" She reached over, patted his cheek, her hand lingering before she removed it. "Those will be your thoughts, Brad. No. Don't get out," she said as Roy held the door for her, then placed her bag on the cart held by the waiting attendant. She quickly leaned over, kissing him hard on his mouth. "Goodbye, Brad." She turned away.

Brad watched her go, her back straight, her head held high, never glancing back as she followed the fast-moving attendant. He stared until she disappeared from view.

Brad sat in his darkened living room watching the snow fall. It was nearly midnight, the night before Christmas Eve day. The day Julia had returned from her trip. The snow had begun falling in early evening with slow but steady flurries. It was soon evident that it was going to stick–the first snowfall of the winter. His stomach burned at the realization. He'd asked himself again and again since the sky became white with the whirling cotton puff, Will she come? After an agonizing two hours, he realized he was waiting in vain. "She did say 'goodbye' after all," he mused aloud, as he poured himself a Hennessy.

He sat in the dark, broodingly waiting for the phone to ring. He had even ordered Chinese food delivered, fearing he'd miss her call. The Scezchuan lobster could have been sawdust for all it mattered. When it became evident that she had no intention of calling, he had become increasingly sullen, hanging up rudely when an acquaintance called inviting him to a Christmas Eve party. He recalled her words to him, their honesty, her sincere admission of her love for him. He ached for her. The thought of never having her beside him, loving him, pulling at the tiny hairs on his chest making him cry out in delicious pain–he moaned, thinking none of these things would be his.

With a swift movement he got up, walked to his bedroom, opened the end table drawer and removed a small box. Opening it, he stared at the glistening gemstone. Snapping the lid closed, he walked to a phone, dialed a number and waited. After barking orders, he hung up.

Now Brad was waiting. He stood up, pensively staring at the

scene just outside his terrace window. The winter landscape on the Bridge appeared as if it were manufactured only for his and Julia's pleasure. It was as they envisioned all those months ago on a sweltering day in July. The tiny cars with red and white lights blinking in the distance moved snail-like across the majestic span. The swirling flakes spun furiously, dancing and twirling and darting as if trying vainly to escape their inevitable final landing; but they came to rest on the slow-moving cars, some finally ending up as the soft white carpet being spoiled by unmerciful wheels.

Leaning casually against the glass doors, hand jammed in his pocket, his eyes narrowed ruefully as he watched the traffic. It had been hours since Roy had appeared at his door, taking the box and a note inside a buff-colored envelope. He'd instructed Roy to wait–but not after midnight.

Julia sat looking at the black opal. The fire danced within the stone as if beckoning to her. She was mesmerized. Her attention shifted to the buff vellum slip of paper she held in her hand. "I love you." The words leapt off the page at Julia. It seemed as if she had been sitting for hours, holding the stone and the note. Ever since the doorman had buzzed Roy up to her apartment around nine p.m., and he had handed her the box, saying, "I'll be downstairs waiting for your reply," she'd been sitting on her overstuffed couch watching the snow fall.

It was nearly midnight when the intercom buzzed. She was told that the driver was still waiting and had asked if there was any message.

"No," she said.

When the snow had started falling earlier that evening, Julia realized that it was the sticking kind. Her heart twinged with emotion. Only yesterday she'd said "goodbye" to Brad and future heartache with him; but when she entered her apartment upon returning from her trip, she prayed to hear his voice on her answering machine. The only messages were invitations to Christmas parties, none of which interested her, not even Jim's reminder to attend his on Christmas Eve.

Woodenly, she had begun unpacking her bag. It didn't take long. She had aimlessly walked about, straightening pillows, swatting at imaginary lint on the sofa, and washing the lone soup bowl and spoon that lay in the sink. Then the doorman had announced Roy's arrival.

Wearily, she pressed her hands against her eyelids for the hundredth time as she stared at the note and the opal and thought about their significance. A small smile appeared at the corner of her mouth. He means it, she thought. He does love me. As if a dark shadow had lifted and dissipated, her eyes shone brightly with unfallen tears.

"He's going to be fine. We're going to be fine." Jumping up off the sofa, she ran to the intercom and pressed a button. When the doorman answered she asked, "Is the driver still there?" Julia yelled excitedly, "Tell him to wait," when the response was "yes."

Crazily she threw off her robe, donning creamed-colored slacks and a matching sweater. Digging out her snow boots, she pulled them on. As she shrugged into her coat, wrapping her scarf around her neck, the phone rang. Ignoring it, not wanting to refuse another party invitation, she grabbed her bag and hat, turning off the lights as she walked to the door. The message finished. There was a pause. Julia waited impatiently, curious about whose party she was not attending. Her hand froze on the doorknob. She shivered when she heard his voice. "I love you, Julia." Fumbling, locking her door, tears rolling down her cheeks, Julia rushed noiselessly down the carpeted hallway to the elevator. The only sound she heard was her thumping heart and Brad's soft voice in her ears.

The light knock at his door brought a frown to Brad's face as he walked toward it. He'd not been informed he was getting a visitor. Opening the door, he stood staring in amazement at Julia, wet snowflakes glistening in her hair, on her hat and on her coat.

"I bribed the doorman," she said with her impish grin. Cocking her head to one side she said, "Well, do I get to come in or are you going to describe the Bridge to me minute by minute?"

Brad reached out, grabbing Julia, crushing her to him. "Oh, God. You're here. Sweet Julia, you came. I love you," he groaned, kissing her eyes, her lips, her forehead. He unbuttoned her coat, tossed off her hat and scarf and crushed her to him again, holding and rocking her in his arms as if he would never release her. He murmured against her damp curls, "My love, my sweet, you came to me. Oh, God."

Julia's arms were wrapped tightly around his waist, her face crushed against his chest. She never wanted to let go. They stood together as if crystallized.

Finally, Julia stirred. Lifting her head she said, "I think maybe we'd better continue this inside . . . if your neighbors are as concerned as mine." Her voice trailed away as Brad grinned, pulling her inside and closing the door. He pushed off her coat, hanging it up in the foyer closet, while Julia slipped out of her boots. Brad, in stockinged feet, guided Julia to the terrace window, his arms tightly around her waist.

She's here, he thought. I'm never letting her go again. Never. His eyes closed and he involuntarily clutched her tighter until he heard her moan. His eyes flew open. Quickly he leaned down, kissing her mouth. Gazing at her, all his love for her shining in his eyes, he spoke. "I'm sorry, sweetheart. I didn't mean to hurt you. It's just that I was thinking that you're never leaving me again. Never." He looked anxiously at her. "Right?"

"Right." She snuggled close, clutching him tightly. "It's even more beautiful than I imagined," she said in awe, watching the winter landscape evolve before her. "It's like a veil . . . a long veil. . . " She and Brad stood for long moments, watching the dancing flakes create a wonderland.

After awhile, Brad murmured against her hair, the sweet smell of her shampoo and the scent of her sending intoxicating shivers down his spine, "I love you, Julia. Don't ever leave me. I want you to be my wife. Will you marry me?"

Julia became still. Her eyes closed and she sighed. Her arm left Brad's waist as she moved from his embrace.

Brad caught his breath as Julia remained silent. His breathing became shallow, his heart nearly stopping as he waited.

His voice was raspy. "If you're not ready for marriage . . . I can understand that. You need some time. But . . . please don't walk away from me. I want you. I'll wait for you . . . but stay with me, Julia." He stared bleakly out the window, his hands clenched in his pockets.

Julia opened her eyes and turned to Brad, tilting her head back to gaze steadily into his eyes.

He gasped. All her love for him was shining there for him to see. He swallowed the lump in his throat, pulling her to him in a bone crushing hug. "You will. You will," he moaned, caressing her cheeks, her eyes, her lips, with his fingers.

"Yes, Brad, I will." She gently pulled herself from his fierce embrace. "I love you. I'll always love you." She held up her hand where the opal shone mysteriously in the pale light. "The stone of prophecy and truth." She kissed him softly. "Somehow, it found us. It will remain with us always. No, my love, I'll never leave you." She reached up putting her hands around his neck and pulling his face to hers. Slowly at first, she kissed him, the long pent-up passion she felt for him unleashing itself finally.

Brad groaned as he strained, trying to capture all the sweetness of her kiss. His hands moved caressingly from the softness of her neck to the gentle swell of her breast, where he slowly slid his thumbs back and forth until he felt the nipples tighten under his touch. Her body, tingling at the sensation, involuntarily arched closer to him. Her senses reeled at the exquisite pain. When Brad's fingers touched her bare skin as they traveled beneath her sweater, the sound escaping her lips was one of pure pleasure. Lifting her arms, she helped Brad ease the garment over her head. Tossing it aside, his hands moved sensuously down her back where he quickly unhooked her bra, allowing the cream-colored lace to fall to the floor. Holding her close once again to his chest, her bare breasts searing him through the fine cotton of his shirt, he called her name as his hands moved gently downward, pressing her hips close to his.

She responded by unbuttoning his shirt and pushing it aside. Placing her mouth over one nipple, she slowly began suckling it.

Drawing in his breath deeply, Brad groaned, "Julia. Oh, my love. I want you."

Julia lifted her head. Her bright, intense gaze held Brad's as she slowly guided his lips to hers. Her kiss was as soft and feathery as the breath of an angel. "You have me, Brad. Forever," she whispered.

A long while later, standing before the window wall, watching the flakes swirl like dervishes in all their glory, they clung to each other, filled with their love.

Julia's eyes sparkled in splendor. "I'm sorry for those with false hearts. If only they could know . . ." Her voice broke.

Brad remembered. He gathered her closely to him, enfolding her gently, his chin resting on her curls. The scent of her was intoxicating. "Yes." Echoing his Paris tale he told her in a low voice, "Only the true hearts can know the magic, my love . . . "

Slowly drawing her down onto the deep couch, enclosed in soft embraces amidst the silvery shadows, they were soon lost in a magic all their own.

Spirit Speaks to Sisters will serve as the standard bearer for books of inspiration and spiritual guidance for decades to come.

$20.95 Hardcover   ISBN 1-878360-39-X

Available at Fine Bookstores Everywhere

INDIGO Series

Sensuous Love Stories For Today's Black Woman

Now Available...

Breeze

Her father, whose life was his music, adored but abandoned her. Her mother, disillusioned with musicians and a bitter life, discouraged and deceived her. Her first love, lost through treachery, returns to teach her the rapture and dangers of unbridled passion. She is successful. She is a superstar. Her name is Breeze.

Love's Deception

Set in the whirlwind corporate world of the Medical Insurance Company, *Love's Deceptions* explores the lives of four women and their explosive relationships with the men in their lives.

Rachel—blessed with beauty and brains, yet trapped in every woman's nightmare...

Lesa—born with a lust for life and a desire for the fast land...

Stacy—a single mother struggling financially makes a decision which could change her life forever...

Mattie—a widow, first devoted to her husband, now devoted to her job...

Everlastin' Love

In 1967, Jaz believed she had everything, a marriage to her high school sweetheart and a secure future. But the Vietnam War caused her fairy tale to end. Jaz was left devastated and alone.

As Jaz struggles to pull her life together, recollections of the past overshadow all attempts at relationships. That is until Kyle Jagger, a coworker, dares her to love again. His patience and unselfish love break through the ghosts of her past, and together they find everlasting love.

Entwined Destinies

Exquisite, prosperous and stunning, Kathy Goodwin had a bright future. Her professional accomplishments as a writer for an international magazine have given her admittance into the most prominent and wealthiest circles. Kathy Goodwin should have had a clear passage to happiness. But, after suffering the tragic death of her parents and the breakup with her fiance, she was withdrawn. Then into Kathy's life comes an extraordinary man, Lloyd Craig, an independent and notable oil company executive. His warm gaze makes her flesh kindle with desire. But Lloyd is tormented by his own demons. Now, they both have to discover the ties that entwine their destinies.

Reckless Surrender

At 29, Rina Matthews' aspirations are coming true...A safe relationship with her business partner...A secure career as an accountant...And, physically, she's more stunning than ever.

Into Rina's life comes the most self-centered but sensuous man she has ever met. Cleveland Whitney is, unfortunately, the son of her most influential client.

While she tries her best to elude him, she's forced to encounter him again and again during a three month assignment in Savannah, Georgia. The handsome lawyer seemed to be deliberately avoiding her...until now. While Cleveland's gaze warms her body, his kisses tantalize, Rina recklessly surrenders to the power of love.

Shades of Desire

Forbidden...Untouchable...Taboo...Clear descriptions of the relationship between Jeremy and Jasmine. Jeremy, tall, handsome and successful...and white. Jasmine, willowy, ravishing and lonely. The attraction is unquestionable, but impossible. Or is it?

Dark Storm Rising

Every time Star Lassiter encounters the wealthy and mysterious African, Duran Ajero, things start to sizzle. It's more than coincidence that he keeps "bumping" into her.

Soon, his charm combined with his hot pursuit of her begins to cause major problems in her life, especially after she meets his sexy live in maid.

Star tries to say "no" in every language she knows, but Duran arrogantly declines to accept her refusals. Sparks continue to fly until they end up stranded at his Delaware beach house...where their passions reach their peak...as the dark storm rises.

Dark Storm Rises...SIZZLES.